MONSIEUR
PAMPLEMOUSSE
INVESTIGATES

MONSIEUR PAMPLEMOUSSE
INVESTIGATES

MICHAEL BOND

FAWCETT COLUMBINE • NEW YORK

A Fawcett Columbine Book

Published by Ballantine Books

Copyright © 1990 by Michael Bond

All rights reserved under International and Pan-American
Copyright Conventions. Published in the United States by
Ballantine Books, a division of Random House, Inc., New
York, and distributed in Canada by Random House of
Canada Limited, Toronto. Originally published in Great
Britain in 1990 by Hodder and Stoughton, a division of
Hodder and Stoughton Limited.

Library of Congress Cataloging-in-Publication Data
Bond, Michael
    Monsieur pamplemousse investigates/
    Michael Bond.—1st American ed.
        p.   cm.
    ISBN 0-449-90527-6
    I. Title.
    PR6052.052M685   1990
    823'.914—dc20   89-92562
Manufactured in the United States of America   CIP

First American Edition: December 1990

10 9 8 7 6 5 4 3 2 1

CONTENTS

THE LAUNCH PARTY

It should have served as an omen. Half-way down the Avenue Junot, while out for his early-morning walk with Pommes Frites, Monsieur Pamplemousse encountered a large black van parked across the pavement outside an apartment block. As he squeezed his way through the tiny gap left between the open rear doors and the entrance to the building, he glanced inside and saw a series of racks running along each wall of the interior. Five of them were filled by leather, coffin-shaped containers. The sixth was empty, awaiting the arrival of another customer.

It was a common enough sight at that time of the year. All the same, it cast a temporary gloom on their outing, a gloom which the leaden clouds almost stationary overhead did nothing to alleviate. Even Pommes Frites hurried on his way as though anxious to put the matter behind him as quickly as possible.

Turning into the Rue Caulaincourt, Monsieur Pamplemousse pulled his jacket collar up to shield his neck from the cold east wind and quickened his pace still further. He wished now he'd worn an overcoat, but at the beginning of the month – much against Madame Pamplemousse's advice – he'd put it away for the year. Pride forbade that he should take it out again, but if the bad weather continued much longer he might have to. March, which had started warm and spring-like, was not going out without a struggle. Every evening the news on the television had fresh tales of woe to tell.

Two sparrows having an early-morning bathe in the water swirling its way down the gutters of the Butte took off when they saw Pommes Frites approaching. A street-cleaning waggon scuttled past like a scalded cat.

Others had their problems too. Pruning had started later than usual in the little vineyard on the nearby slopes of Montmartre, and the tables and chairs which would normally have appeared by now in the Place du Tertre ready for the tourist season were still under cover. The Easter eggs in the window of the *boulangerie* looked premature.

Carrying a bag of breakfast supplies and a copy of the morning *journal*, Monsieur Pamplemousse retraced his steps back up the hill. He took a short cut this time – up the Rue Simon Dereure and through the little park opposite his apartment. It was a truncated version of what he called 'the round', but it was no morning for lingering.

Armed with a pointed stick, the park-keeper was doing his rounds, prodding at sleeping figures tucked away in odd corners, sheltering from the wind.

Out of respect for their plight, Monsieur Pamplemousse looked the other way. Windows on the upper floors of sur- rounding buildings were being flung open as women ap- peared and began draping bedclothes across their balcony railings to be aired. Some children were already hard at work on the slides in the play area, their downward progress slowed by the morning dew.

If it weren't for all the cars parked at the sides of the roads, Montmartre in the early morning wasn't so far removed from the way it must have been when Utrillo painted it.

Waiting by the Boules area for Pommes Frites he remem- bered the encounter with the van and wondered if perhaps there would be one player less that afternoon. One thing was certain: it wouldn't stop the game. Nothing short of an earthquake would ever do that.

Back home again, Monsieur Pamplemousse found *café* already percolating on the stove and a glass of freshly squeezed orange juice beside his plate. Pommes Frites slaked his thirst noisily from a bowl of water and then collapsed in a heap on a rug under the kitchen table while he waited for his *petit déjeuner*.

Distributing his purchases, a *croissant* on the opposite plate, and a *pain au sucre* for himself, Monsieur Pamplemousse settled down and glanced through the *journal* while he waited for Doucette to join him.

It was the usual mixture of gloom and despondency; news of the weather still predominated. He sometimes wondered why he bothered to read it, except that the day always felt incomplete without at least a cursory glance through the headlines, and he was about to discard it when his eye alighted on a brief entry amongst a list of recent bereavements. It stood out from the rest by virtue of being in bolder type. For a moment or two he could scarcely believe his eyes. Then he jumped to his feet.

'*Sacrebleu*! It is not possible!'

'What is not possible?' Madame Pamplemousse, her hair still in rollers, bustled in from the bedroom. 'You are forever telling me all things are possible.'

'The Director is *mort*!'

'What? I don't believe it!' Madame Pamplemousse automatically crossed herself.

He handed her the *journal*. 'Look for yourself.'

She scanned the entry briefly and then handed the *journal* back to him. 'Poof! It is typical. They cannot even get the date right.'

Stifling his irritation, Monsieur Pamplemousse re-read the item. It was also typical of Doucette that she should fasten on some minor detail and in so doing, lose sight of the whole. What did it matter if it was today's date, yesterday's date, or even, as in the present case, a whole week away? Which was also, by sheer coincidence, the third Tuesday in March, traditionally publication day of *Le Guide*. The fact that she was right did nothing to soften the blow. The printer's error was a trivial matter by comparison. Perhaps the compositor responsible had recognised the name and gone into a state of shock, emotion dulling his skills. There were a hundred possible explanations. The important fact was that the Director, the head of France's oldest and most respected food guide, was no longer with them. Blinds in restaurants the length and

9

breadth of the Republic would be lowered; flags across the nation would be flown at half-mast.

He lifted the telephone receiver and dialled his office number. Not surprisingly, it was engaged. The switchboard was probably awash with incoming calls.

'It would happen today of all days.'

'If you're dead, you're dead.' Madame Pamplemousse reached for the *café*. 'It doesn't make any difference which day it is. Will you care which day it is when it happens to you? I certainly shan't.'

'Today, Couscous,' said Monsieur Pamplemousse simply, 'happens to be the very day when the text for the new edition of *Le Guide* is being sent to the printers. It is what we have all been working for over the past year. There was to have been the usual send-off party . . . '

'It will still go to the printers.'

'*Oui*, Couscous, it will still go. But it will not be the same.'

There wouldn't be the Director's speech for a start. Every year they all assembled in the boardroom – office staff, Inspectors, everyone connected with the production – and there was a buffet lunch. Apart from the annual staff outing in Normandy, it was the one occasion in the year when they all got together and were able to swop reminiscences and talk about the things that had happened to them over the past year. Often it went on far into the night.

'At least you'll be home early for a change, *and* you'll be spared the speech. You've always said that once the Director gets going there's no stopping him.'

Monsieur Pamplemousse finished his *pain au sucre* and rose from the table. 'I must change. I can't go looking like this.' There was no point in discussing the matter. Either you understood these things or you didn't. It was really a case of rhythms. Some things that were said half-jokingly in life did not bear repeating after death. Often the things that seemed tedious at the time were the things you missed most of all.

'You'll find your black suit in a plastic bag behind the vacuum cleaner. I had it cleaned after you went to your Tante Mathilde's funeral last May.'

He looked out of the bedroom window. Was it his imagination, or were the clouds even darker than they had been earlier? He shivered. His winter suit felt stiff after his comfortable, lived-in clothes. It also smelled of mothballs, but at least the material was warm.

He still could hardly believe the news. It was only a matter of weeks since he'd last seen the Director and he'd been looking unusually hale and hearty then. A trifle overweight perhaps, but weren't they all? It was an occupational hazard. On an impulse he went into the bathroom and stepped on the scales, then wished he hadn't. Even allowing for the fact that his suit was made of heavy material, it was still not good news.

Pommes Frites was waiting for him when he came out of the bathroom. He had a black bow tied to his collar and his coat had been freshly brushed.

'Take care.' Doucette came to the door and kissed him goodbye. 'If you speak to *Monsieur le Directeur*'s wife, do tell her how sorry I am.' Monsieur Pamplemousse gave her a squeeze. Bad news took people in different ways. He knew that deep down she was really very upset.

He gave a final wave as the lift doors started to close. '*A bientôt.*'

'I will expect you when I see you.' It was a throw-away remark, although had he but known, it would echo in his ears for days to come. In any case he had too many things running through his mind to do more than give an answering nod.

Who would take over the running of *Le Guide* for a start? It was impossible to picture anyone new. As far as he was concerned the Director had always been there. They had enjoyed a special relationship, too; a relationship which dated back to his days in the *Sûreté*. He had once done the Director a favour while working on a case, and it had later borne fruit, when he had found himself forced into early retirement and by a stroke of good fortune they had bumped into each other again. If it hadn't been for that chance meeting he wouldn't have landed a job with *Le Guide*.

He paused at the top of the steps leading down to the

Lamarck-Caulaincourt Métro, then spotted a taxi waiting in the rank further down the road. It would save any possible arguments with ticket collectors over Pommes Frites' size. Like most of the other Inspectors, he had taken advantage of the lunch party to put his car in for a service. Now he was beginning to regret the decision.

It was also ironic that the Director should pass away at this particular time – just as they were about to be computerised. Under his management *Le Guide* had always been in the forefront of the latest scientific developments. It was like France itself in a way – on the one hand, firmly rooted in the best traditions of the past, on the other, paying homage at the altar of progress, and long may it remain so.

Perhaps because of the strong smell of mothballs, the driver pointedly opened his window. Once again Monsieur Pamplemousse regretted his lack of an overcoat. Pommes Frites, ever-sensitive to his master's moods, looked suitably put out as he gazed at the passing scene.

The decision to commit the entire guide to a computer had not been taken lightly. It was undoubtedly a logical step if they were to keep one step ahead of their competitors, but given the vast number of entries and the immense amount of information which flowed into *Le Guide*'s headquarters every day of the year, information which needed to be collated and analysed, weighed and debated upon before it was programmed, it was also a mind-boggling task. As he'd said to Doucette: a year's work. And there were rumours that other innovations were about to be unveiled. It was a shame the Director wouldn't be there to announce them.

As they crossed the Pont de l'Alma and swung round in a wide arc in order to circumnavigate the Place de la Résistance, Monsieur Pamplemousse asked the driver to stop when he had a suitable opportunity. It wasn't so much that he needed the walk, it was more a matter of composing himself before he reached the office. A quiet stroll along the bank of the Seine would do him good.

Half-way along the Quai d'Orsay he overtook one of his colleagues, Glandier, obviously doing the same thing.

Glandier shook hands as he came up alongside. 'A bad business.'

'Unbelievable.'

'If you ask me,' said Glandier gloomily, 'there's a jinx on the place. What with last week . . . '

'Last week?'

'You mean, you haven't heard?'

Monsieur Pamplemousse shook his head. 'I've been on the road for the last month.'

Glandier gave a hollow laugh. 'You missed all the fun. Someone put a piranha fish in the fountain outside the main entrance. There was hell to pay.'

Monsieur Pamplemousse whistled. 'What happened?'

'It ate all the goldfish for a start. Then it nearly did for one of the typists. Apparently she was sitting on the side having her *déjeuner*. She only put her hand in the water for a split second, and . . . whoosh!'

'Whoosh! Is she . . . ?'

Glandier raised his hand and waggled it from side to side. '*Comme ci, comme ça.* Poof! Luckily she was wearing gloves. She has regained the power of speech, but it's probably put her off sandwiches for life.'

As they turned into the Esplanade des Invalides Monsieur Pamplemousse spotted a row of large grey vans parked at the far end of the Rue Fabert. Cables were snaked across the pavement. A man wearing headphones waved a clipboard to someone inside the courtyard of *Le Guide*'s headquarters.

'They are here already!'

Both men quickened their pace until they drew level with the first of the vans, when they were suddenly stopped dead in their tracks. An open door revealed an outside-broadcast control-room, and they could just see a row of television screens showing varying shots of the same subject. Unmistakably, that subject was the Director himself.

'It must be an old film. I'm not sure I want to see it.'

Glandier was about to go on his way when Monsieur Pamplemousse stopped him.

'*Attendez!*' He pushed a path through a small knot of

13

sightseers gathered on the pavement.

Above the hum of generators and the barking of orders from a producer seated in front of a control panel, they clearly heard snatches of a familiar voice.

' . . . deeply grateful for the concern everyone has shown . . . a foolish prank on the part of someone as yet unidentified . . . as you can see . . . no, it is *not* a publicity stunt . . . ' The picture on the largest of the monitors – one labelled TRANSMISSION – changed to a tight close-up of the Director looking angry at the thought. '*Le Guide* has never had need for such things, nor, whilst I remain in charge, will it ever.'

The rest was drowned by a round of applause. The camera zoomed out and the picture on the monitor changed to a studio shot. The interview was over. Everyone in the van relaxed.

'*Sapristi!* What do you make of it?' Glandier hurried after Monsieur Pamplemousse as he led the way towards the entrance to *Le Guide*'s headquarters. 'I'll tell you something for nothing. There's bound to be another mishap. Things always go in threes.'

The big double gates were open and the inner courtyard was crowded with people; the television crew, already dismantling their equipment ready for the next assignment, had given way to hordes of reporters and press photographers. Standing at the top of the steps leading to the main entrance was the erect figure of the Director. He appeared to be making the most of the situation: head back, chin out, right hand thrust beneath one lapel of his jacket, he looked for all the world as though he was giving an impersonation of Napoleon addressing his troops prior to giving the off signal for their historic crossing of the Alps.

Beyond the huge plate-glass doors Monsieur Pamplemousse could see rows of familiar faces pressed against the glass. Like himself, many of those present were dressed in black. Word must have spread like wildfire.

The battery of discharging flash-guns and the accompanying volley of clicking shutters would have been more than enough to satisfy even the most unpopular member of government hoping to achieve re-election; no film star seeking publicity for her current extravaganza would have had any cause to complain. Certainly the Director himself looked far from displeased as he gave a final wave to the news-hungry crowd before disappearing into the building.

'So much for the anonymity of *Le Guide*,' said Glandier.

Monsieur Pamplemousse gave a grunt. 'He's probably right. Get it all over in one fell swoop. There's nothing more dangerous than an unsatisfied reporter.'

All the same, he knew what Glandier meant. Entry to the hallowed forecourt was normally only achieved by means of a magnetic card issued solely to employees of *Le Guide*. Even then, they had to pass the scrutiny of old Rambaud, the commissionaire, who had been there for longer than anyone else could remember. This furore would probably give him nightmares for weeks to come.

As they entered the building, the Director detached himself from a group congregated near the reception desk and drew Monsieur Pamplemousse to one side.

'I've been trying to get hold of you, Pamplemousse,' he complained, in the accusing tone of voice peculiar to those whose attempts to make contact with someone by telephone have been unsuccessful.

'I called as soon as I heard the news, *Monsieur*,' said Monsieur Pamplemousse defensively. 'All lines were engaged.' It was not his fault if Doucette had gone out shopping.

'It is an infuriating business. I shall not rest until I get to the bottom of it. If I discover the culprit is a member of the staff . . . ' The rest was left to the imagination.

'You think it is someone within *Le Guide*, *Monsieur*?'

'I can think of no other possible explanation. Michelin wouldn't stoop to such a thing. Besides, they have already sent their condolences in the form of a red rocking-chair made out of poppies. A singular honour, particularly as I am told poppies are out of season. And Gault-Millau may have their eccentricities, but I can't believe they would be capable of perpetrating something so juvenile. They have denied all

15

knowledge.'

'Have you enquired of the *journal* concerned, *Monsieur*?'

'I have indeed. I spoke with the editor at length soon after the news broke. Apparently the entry was placed over the telephone late yesterday evening by someone purporting to be the proprietor. It was dealt with by a junior who has, I gather, already departed for pastures new.

'Once today is over, Pamplemousse, I want you to take charge of the investigation. It needs someone with a finger on the pulse of the organisation, someone skilled in the art of keeping a discreet ear to the ground, whilst at the same time possessed of a nose for the scent of untoward behaviour. Your past training will be invaluable.'

Monsieur Pamplemousse absorbed this news with something less than enthusiasm. Apart from the dubious mechanics of the Director's roll-call of his talents, which made the task ahead sound more suited to Pommes Frites, he had no wish to become embroiled in a situation which could well result in ill-feeling from the rest of the staff if they felt he was prying into their affairs.

However, any protests he might have voiced were rendered stillborn as the Director departed in order to prepare himself for his annual speech.

Monsieur Pamplemousse joined in the general throng making their way up to the boardroom on the fourth floor – some by lift, others, like himself, by the central staircase. In a matter of moments he was deep into shaking hands, greeting old friends and making new ones; Truffert asked to be reminded later to relate the story of an adventure he'd had on the Orient Express; Guilot, still persisting with his diet of fresh carrot juice before all meals, and clearly ignoring his weight problem for the day, was looking positively orange; Daladier had stumbled across a new restaurant near Strasbourg, which for the area he rated second only to that of the Haeberlin brothers; Trigaux in the art department – busily recording the event with his camera for *L'Escargot*, the staff magazine – had a new piece of photographic equipment he wanted to show Monsieur Pamplemousse when he had time.

The catering department had excelled themselves. It was their one moment of glory in the year, a chance to demonstrate that their skills extended beyond Tuesday's *cassoulet* and Friday's inevitable *ragoût*. *Pâtés* vied with each other alongside an array of cold meats and salads; there was one table devoted entirely to fish and another to meat; tureens full of as yet undisclosed delights simmered away on a fourth. There was a display of cheese on a fifth followed by a tempting display of *desserts* for those who managed to stay the course.

Champagne greeted them as they entered the room, while on other tables at the far end were gathered an assortment of bottles to delight both the eye and the palate. Without straining too much, Monsieur Pamplemousse picked out and mentally earmarked a Bâtard-Montrachet from Remoissenet and a Charmes-Chambertin bearing the illustrious name of Dujac. On another table there was an impressive collection of old Armagnacs and Cognacs.

Given the fact that most of those present were in various degrees of mourning, ranging from a mere armband to total blackness (and those in the former category clearly regretted they hadn't taken more trouble over their dress; the Director had an eye for such things), it looked more like a convention of undertakers getting together after an unusually successful year than a gathering of hungry gourmets anxious to do justice to what lay before them.

Monsieur Pamplemousse wished now he'd been less optimistic about his chances of returning home early. He looked round, weighing up the possibility of slipping back outside in order to make a quick phone call to Doucette – he could tell her the good news about the Director at the same time – but the crush of people following on behind made it hardly worth contemplating.

Glandier clinched matters by handing him a plate.

'We shall suffer for this,' he murmured. 'But what suffering! I'm glad I've got a late pass back at the works.'

Reminded of his responsibilities by a pressure against his

right leg, Monsieur Pamplemousse picked up another plate for Pommes Frites.

As he moved slowly along the succession of tables, listening to the conversation and the laughter coming from all sides, it was hard to picture there being a Judas in the camp. If such a person existed, he – or she – would be very well fed. Well fed, and ungrateful to boot. The Director might have his faults, but no one could possibly complain of being badly treated. Goodness knows what the lunch must have cost. He wouldn't like to have to foot the bill.

The thought triggered off another. So far he hadn't set eyes on Madame Grante. As Head of Accounts she was usually at the forefront of things, keeping an eagle eye on all that went on. Truffert had a theory she checked their portions and made it up afterwards when it came to going through their expense sheets. He glanced around, but she was nowhere to be seen.

Feeling suddenly in need of a little peace and quiet, Monsieur Pamplemousse made his way to the far end of the room and found himself a chair near the dais from which the Director would be making his speech later that afternoon. On the platform there was a lectern and a small table on which reposed a glass and an ominously large bottle of Badoit. To the rear there was another table bearing an object covered in a shroud from beneath which there emerged a cable connected to a wall socket.

Gradually the hubbub died down as talk gave way to the serious business of eating. Waiters in fawn-coloured uniform embroidered with replicas of Le Guide's symbol – two escargots rampant – moved discreetly to and fro amongst the crowd, charging and recharging glasses.

If the Bâtard-Montrachet was grand and sumptuous, the Charmes-Chambertin was elegance personified; each was more than worthy of the occasion and both improved as the afternoon wore on. All in all, by the time the Director made his entrance, Monsieur Pamplemousse felt at peace with the world. His only regret was that he'd seated himself in a position from which there was patently no escape, right next to the dais. A quiet sleep was out of the question; a noisy one even more so. It was worse than being back at school. He wished now he'd stuck with Glandier.

'I do not propose,' began the Director, holding up one hand for silence, 'to dwell on this morning's events, nor do I intend to speculate on the possible motivation for what on the surface would seem to be an utterly senseless and irresponsible action.'

Monsieur Pamplemousse suppressed a groan. He knew the signs. When the Director said he wasn't going to dwell on something it usually meant quite the opposite. They were in for a long peroration. He hoped Pommes Frites behaved. One year, when some unidentified person had laced his water bowl with *vin rouge*, he had disgraced himself by snoring loudly during a particularly long and boring passage.

Monsieur Pamplemousse half-closed his eyes and placed one hand on his forehead in what he hoped would be interpreted as a look of deep concentration.

It was a very strange business and no mistake. If it was a practical joke, then it was in dubious taste and must have caused more heartaches than laughter. Hoaxes were all very well in their way, but there were limits.

Having relieved himself of his feelings on the subject of the morning's events, the Director devoted the first part of his speech to the usual statistics relating to the past year's activities. Out of over fifty thousand restaurants and hotels currently listed in the archives, less than ten thousand had found their way into *Le Guide*. That was not a denigration of those establishments who failed to gain entry, rather a pointer to *Le Guide*'s very high standards. Standards which, in a world where the very currency of the word was tending to become more and more debased, they must endeavour to maintain regardless of the cost. Reputations took years to build up; they could be destroyed overnight.

Out of the nine thousand eight hundred and twenty-three restaurants mentioned, eighteen had been singled out for the supreme accolade of three Stock Pots, eighty-one would receive two Stock Pots – a change in an upward direction of three over the previous year – and five hundred and nineteen were being awarded one Stock Pot. Congratulatory telexes were being prepared.

There were the usual moments of light relief. Reference was made to how many kilometres of *saucisses* and *saucissons* had been consumed by Inspectors in the course of duty. There were statistics relating to car mileage, the amount of wine drunk, and a pointed reference to the percentage rise in claims for expenses.

In proposing the usual vote of thanks to Madame Grante for her painstaking preparation of the figures, the Director raised a hollow laugh when he said that despite constant research a machine had yet to be perfected which would in any way replace her. Someone at the back of the room – it sounded like Truffert – triggered off a titter by shouting '*Quel dommage!*' It was instantly quelled by a strong glare from the Director.

Monsieur Pamplemousse looked round the room again, but there was still no sign of Madame Grante. Perhaps, despite the Director's words, she had taken umbrage. People were very resistant to change when their own jobs were threatened, and he'd heard rumours to the effect that all was not well in her department.

'We come now,' continued the Director, 'to the moment in the afternoon you have doubtless all been waiting for. I refer, of course, to the decision we made last year to enter the computer age.

'It was a decision, I need hardly tell you, which was not arrived at without a great deal of heart searching. *Le Guide* has always prided itself on its efficiency and in being in the forefront of all the latest scientific and managerial develop-ments. In the past our unique filing system has been the envy of many of our rivals. However, in recent years we have been falling behind. We can no longer afford to ignore either the march of progress or the benefits which the coming of the computer has conferred on those who have acquired one. Information is our working capital, and anything which enables us to draw on that capital and make use of it quickly and efficiently can only be for the good.

'There are those who would say that we should have made the move much sooner. To them I would point out that part of our strength has always been those very same qualities which I believe make France the country it is: the will and the ability and the enthusiasm to embrace the new whilst still retaining the best of the old. We have merely taken time to make sure we are balancing the two often conflicting forces in order to achieve a harmonious whole.

'There was a time when computers were surrounded in mystery. Only highly trained operators were allowed anywhere near them, and they became the "élite" – the "high priests" as it were, acquiring power previously reserved for the higher echelons. Then, as so often happens, things turned full circle. Now, with the coming of the microcomputer, power in many companies has been transferred yet again, but this time to anyone capable of operating a keyboard. Both situations have their drawbacks and their hazards. The one is like a ship with a member of the crew who usurps the captain's position but is never seen; the other is like a ship where every member of the crew thinks he is capable of running it.

'I wish to say here and now that Le Guide will have but one captain. I intend to remain firmly at the helm.'

The Director took advantage of the sustained applause which greeted this last remark to help himself to a glass of Badoit.

'It is our intention to combine the best of both worlds. We have installed a central computer large enough, and powerful enough, to see us into the next century. On one level it will take care of all the information necessary to produce Le Guide, and this information will be accessed by only a few, thus guarding our reputation for anonymity and total secrecy. On another level it will provide us with ample facilities for the many other uses we intend putting it to. Our public information service will be enhanced. Our accounting system will be updated. Our reference library will become second to none. The list of potential benefits is almost endless.

'Concurrent with this technological leap, the first of the major changes I have to announce concerns *Le Guide*'s system of symbols; a system which, although it has amply withstood the test of time, is now in need of reassessment in order to take account of modern developments and changes in social behaviour. Over the past few years we have received many complaints, particularly from our older readers, about the problem of background music in restaurants. The most common argument advanced, and one which I have to admit strikes a chord of sympathy, is that if people feel like sharing their meal with a military band then they should take a picnic lunch in the Champs-Elysées on Bastille Day. Most people go to a restaurant in order to enjoy a meal in peace and quiet, not to have their ears assailed by discordant cacophonies from a battery of ill-concealed loudspeakers. Accordingly, we intend to institute a symbol of ear-plugs rampant for those establishments which come under the heading of "persistent offenders".

'There are to be other new symbols which you will learn about in due course – an unshaded *luminaire* for a low standard of ambience is but one example; others will be introduced in the fullness of time, but slowly, so as not to place too great a burden on you all.'

Aware that the buzz of conversation following his pronouncement had not entirely subsided and that a good part of his audience had seized on the chance to relax, the Director raised his voice.

'I come now to the major event of the afternoon. We have decided to institute a new award which I believe will be unique in the annals of catering. It will be in the form of a golden Stock Pot lid and will be presented annually to the best restaurant in France. The winner will then hold it for a year. There will, of course, be similar awards for the runners-up. A silver lid for the second and a bronze lid for the third.

'A few moments ago I made reference to our system of awarding Stock Pots to those restaurants who merit it, restaurants where the cuisine, the surroundings and the service are all exceptional and justify a special journey, much as

Michelin award their stars and Gault-Millau their toques. As you all know, other guides have different systems again, none of which are entirely without merit.

'However, admirable though all these awards are, the one criticism one may level at them – our own included – is that in the final analysis they are still subjective and as such are open to human errors and human frailties; judgements can become clouded – over-indulgence by an Inspector the previous evening, indisposition of the chef on the day itself – the possibilities are endless.

'In order to arrive at a fair, indeed one might almost call it an incontrovertible decision as to which is the very best restaurant in the whole of France, and therefore, almost by definition, the whole of the world, I have decided to take full advantage of our latest acquisition. All this week staff have been busy feeding the computer with every scrap of information obtained over the past year and even while I have been talking it has been sifting this material, digesting and dissecting it, annotating the result, weighing one factor not simply against another, but against many thousand of others. It is a task which I am told would take a hundred skilled mathematicians many months to complete. And yet,' the Director turned and like a magician presenting his *pièce de résistance*, removed the shroud from the object behind him with a flourish, 'such is the miracle of modern science, the answer will be printed out the moment I issue the appropriate command on the keyboard you see in front of you; a keyboard which is connected to the mainframe in our computer room in another part of the building. I, myself, do not as yet know the result – no one does – but I can assure you that it will be as accurate and as unbiased as man could possibly devise.'

Ever one to extract the last soupçon of drama from a situation, the Director paused with one finger poised above the keyboard for long enough to allow a total hush to fall over the room. Then, at exactly the right moment, he struck, tapping out a series of instructions at a speed which would have earned him a place in the typing pool any day of the week and which must have taken many hours of rehearsal.

There was a moment of total silence, the barest fraction of a second, then a red lamp winked and a series of bleeps issued from the command module. The printer emitted an answering buzz and as it leapt into life a daisy-wheel rattled out its response like a machine-gun.

From his vantage point near the front, Monsieur Pamplemousse tried to calculate the possibilities, but it was a hopeless task. It was obviously too short for his own nomination – Les Cinq Parfaits, near Evian. It was more than one word so it couldn't be Taillevant, or Bocuse. It was too long for Pic or Chapel. La Mère Blanc at Vézelay perhaps?

Once again the Director appeared to be milking the situation for all it was worth. As a sheet of paper emerged from the machine, he tore it off and held it up to the light while his audience waited with baited breath.

They waited in vain. The Director turned white. His lips moved, but gave vent only to a strange choking noise. Clutching at the lectern for support, he slid sideways in a kind of spiralling motion, taking everything with him.

The resultant explosion of sound as both Director and microphone landed on the floor together, amplified by many decibels, produced a momentary state of shock in those nearest to the dais. A second later there was a forward rush to go to his aid. In the excitement the piece of paper he'd been clutching floated to the floor unheeded, save by Pommes Frites who, thinking it was perhaps some new kind of game, reached out his paw. Monsieur Pamplemousse retrieved the sheet before the worst happened. As he scanned the only typewritten words it bore, he too went white.

'Tell us the worst.' It was Glandier.

Monsieur Pamplemousse handed him the paper in silence, unable to bring himself to speak. He wished he'd let Pommes Frites do whatever he'd wanted to do with it.

Glandier whistled. 'No wonder the old man threw a wobbly.'

'Have you ever heard of it?'

'The Wun Pooh? I've *heard* of it. It's a Chinese take-away in Dieppe. It's supposed to be very popular with day-trippers

24

from England. They go there on the way back from their shopping expeditions. Don't you remember? There was all that fuss last year.'

Now that Glandier reminded him, Monsieur Pamplemousse remembered it all too well. Half a ferry-boat had gone down with food poisoning.

'I told you there'd be a third thing,' said Glandier gloomily as he handed back the paper. 'But if you ask me this is the third, fourth, fifth and sixth, all rolled into one. So much for computerisation. If that's what it's come up with it means the end of civilisation as we know it. Talk about micro-chips with everything! I'm going to get myself a pick-me-up. How about you?'

Monsieur Pamplemousse shook his head. Folding the paper carefully in two, he placed it in an inside pocket. Much as he would have liked to join Glandier in a drink, or even two, it was as well to keep a clear head.

In a land where the possibilities for earning an award for culinary distinction were endless and the candidates almost without number, a Chinese take-away in Dieppe had to be fairly low on the list of hopefuls. To nominate it for what promised to be France's premier trophy had to be some kind of joke. It was black humour at its very worst.

Instinct told him that his services were likely to be called for in the not-too-distant future, and when that happened he was going to need every last gramme of stone-cold reasoning he could muster.

2

BYTES AND RAMS

'Pamplemousse, I hope I never have to live through another
day like today.' The Director screwed up a sheaf of computer
paper, tossed it into a nearby waste-paper bin, and then ran
his hand through hair already ruffled by previous encounters.

Monsieur Pamplemousse exchanged a glance with the Staff
Nurse as she clicked her case shut and made to leave. One
look said it all. The Director must have been giving her a hard
time. It showed too, in the state of his office. Normally it was
like its incumbent, a model of all that was neat and tidy.
There was rarely a paper out of place. Flowers stood to
attention in their vases. Now it looked as though a hurricane
had recently passed through, leaving in its wake a trail of
debris picked up *en route* and then discarded. As for the
Director himself, his once immaculately knotted tie hung like
a hangman's noose about his neck, his jacket had fallen to the
floor and his face was ashen.

'May I refill your glass, *Monsieur*?' It was a superfluous
question. The Director handed it to him automatically, then
leaned back in his chair.

'Help yourself while you're there. I'm sure you must be in
need of one too.'

'Thank you, *Monsieur*, but no.'

'Ah, Aristide, I wish I had your strength of character.'

Monsieur Pamplemousse didn't deny himself the pleasure
of the compliment, although it was self-preservation rather
than strength of character that dictated his refusal. He'd said
no for the same reason that he had denied Glandier's offer.
He wished to keep a clear head. The wisdom of his earlier

26

decision had been confirmed shortly afterwards when he received an urgent but not entirely unexpected summons to the top floor.

He took the Director's glass and crossed to the drinks cupboard. The interior light was on and a half-empty bottle of Cognac stood on the shelf. Perhaps on second thoughts it was only half-full. Why did the first way of putting it always sound so much worse than the second, and why did one invariably choose the first? He picked it up and looked at the label. It was a Roullet *Très Rare Hors d'Age*. The Director didn't stint himself.

Monsieur Pamplemousse felt as if the founder of *Le Guide*, Monsieur Hippolyte Duval, was watching him as he poured a generous helping. Hanging on the wall above the cupboard, it was one of those paintings where the eyes of the subject seem to follow the viewer everywhere. Monsieur Pamplemousse couldn't but reflect that their illustrious founder would be turning in his grave if he had only half an inkling of what was going on. No doubt, were he able to see it, his disapproval would also extend to a computer terminal on its dark grey stand to one side of the drinks cabinet. Even the presence alongside the keyboard of Messieurs Cocks et Féret's tome-like but indispensable 1,800-page compendium of the wines of Bordeaux – *Bordeaux et ses Vins* – would hardly have put him in a better frame of mind. It seemed to be doing service as a paper-weight.

As Monsieur Pamplemousse glanced up at the painting, he gave a start. Monsieur Duval was now sporting a long black beard reaching almost down to his waist.

'*Qu'est-ce que c'est?*'

'You may well ask, Pamplemousse.' The Director held up a large felt-tipped pen. 'To rub salt into the wound, whoever was responsible used one of my own implements to perpetrate the deed.' He dismissed the affair with a wave of his hand. 'Graffiti can be erased – resetting *Le Guide* is another matter entirely.'

'Can the error not be put right, *Monsieur*? Surely that is the beauty of having everything on a computer . . . '

The Director gave a groan. 'Would that were so, Pample-mousse. The engineers have been and gone. There is nothing they can do. It has been completely reprogrammed. They are "looking into it", and we all know what that means.'

Monsieur Pamplemousse returned to the Director's desk and handed him the glass. The Director swallowed the contents in one go. Clearly he was in a bad way. 'Pamplemousse . . . ask me who won the silver award.'

'Who won the silver award, *Monsieur*?'

'The Restaurant de la Gare in Mougins!'

'The Restaurant de la Gare in Mougins? But that is crazy! For a start there is no *Gare* in Mougins. There isn't even a railway in Mougins. The nearest *Gare* is at Cannes.'

'I know, Aristide. I know. There is no need to remind me.'

'And what about the Moulin de Mougins, *Monsieur*? That is one of France's premier restaurants. It has boasted three Stock Pots for as long as I can remember. Why . . . '

'According to our entry it has been relegated to a mere bar stool – the symbol we have always reserved for those wayside cafés where one is assured of a good snack. Even worse, there is an additional note saying, "They should try harder." Vergé will be livid. He will undoubtedly seek legal advice.'

'And the bronze Stock Pot lid?'

'It has gone to our own canteen. Much as I like to encourage them in their endeavours, it makes a mockery of the whole thing. Apart from which it savours of nepotism.'

'And the rest of the book, *Monsieur*?'

'*Désastre*!' The Director reached down, picked up a seemingly never-ending length of computer print-out material and allowed it to slide through his fingers to the floor. '*Le Guide* is riddled from beginning to end with entries which are such a travesty of all they are meant to convey they are positively obscene; the Tour d'Argent is slated for the quality of its duck, Pic for his miserly portions, Chapel for being over-addicted to the cruet . . . Need I continue?'

Monsieur Pamplemousse shook his head. He could see now why the Director was in such a state. The last time he'd had a meal at Pic he hadn't wanted to eat for days afterwards, and he'd once been present at Chapel when some other diners – a group of tourists – had asked for the salt. They had been shown the door immediately. *Le Guide* prided itself on the accuracy of its entries; the finding of a single misprint was spoken of in hushed tones for days afterwards. When it happened, which was rarely, heads were apt to roll; annual increments were set at risk. But blatant misinformation was something else again. It didn't bear thinking about. The only consolation was that the master disk hadn't gone to the printers. The thought triggered off another.

'I hesitate to mention it, *Monsieur*, but surely there must be a copy of the original somewhere – a duplicate?'

'Pamplemousse . . . ' the Director gestured towards a pile of paper on the floor, 'you are looking at the print-out from the copy. It is the same as the original. That was the first thing I thought of. As you well know, *Le Guide* has always believed in a belt and braces approach to matters of importance. Unfortunately, we failed to make a copy of the copy. Whoever perpetrated this outrage left no stone unturned.'

'And how about insurance, *Monsieur*?'

'You cannot insure against loss of confidence, Aristide. No policy in the world will cover that.'

The Director rose from his desk and crossed to the doors leading to his balcony. He opened them and went outside. For a moment or two he stood leaning over the parapet, gazing into space. Fearing the worst, Monsieur Pamplemousse hurried out to join him. Beyond the Seine, the late afternoon sun broke through a gap in the clouds and momentarily illuminated the dome of the Sacré-Coeur; to their left the Eiffel Tower cast its long shadow over the surrounding houses; to their right there were men playing Boules on the gravelled perimeter of the Parc du Champ-de-Mars. Each in its own way was a symbol of the unchanging pattern of life; both a solace and sharp reminder of their own precarious situation. The Director must have felt it too, for as he turned away he gave a little shiver.

'Never, not once in its history, Aristide, has *Le Guide* been late for publication. It must not, indeed *will* not happen now.

I have been in consultation with the printers and the very latest they can hold the presses and still meet our deadline is next Friday – three days from now. It means you will need to work fast. I shall prepare a statement for the media in case the worst happens, but I trust that with your help we shall not need it.'

Monsieur Pamplemousse gave a start. It hadn't occurred to him that the Director wanted to see him for anything more than some passing advice. The name of the right person to contact in the *Sûreté*, perhaps; an expert in what was known as 'hacking', for clearly they were dealing not just with a simple fault of programming, but rather an act of deliberate sabotage.

'Surely, *Monsieur*, this is a matter for the police? I know nothing about computers.'

'The police!' The Director gazed at him in horror. 'The police are the last people I wish to involve, Pamplemousse. As you must know only too well, if we bring in the police word is bound to get out. With all due respect to your past profession, I doubt very much if they are equipped to deal with this kind of situation; they are bound to seek outside advice and the more people who know the harder it will be to maintain secrecy. Someone will drop a hint to the wrong person and once the story is out reporters will descend on us again like a flock of vultures. You saw what happened this morning. They will not rest until our collective bones have been picked clean. We shall be the laughing stock of the culinary world. *Le Guide*'s credibility will be destroyed forever.'

'But, *Monsieur* . . . '

His protestations fell on deaf ears. The Director dismissed them with a wave of the hand. 'I do not wish to hear another word, Aristide. For whatever reason, someone has embarked on a policy clearly aimed at the destruction of *Le Guide*. The acts already carried out – the piranha fish in the fountain, that ridiculous announcement in today's *journal* about my demise, the beard now adorning the face of our founder – were but warning salvoes. Were he – or she – to be successful in their endeavours, then ruination will stare us all in the face. It is a matter for the Security Officer.'

'Ah, I had not realised we have a Security Officer.' Monsieur Pamplemousse tried to keep the note of relief from his voice. For a brief moment he had feared the worst.

'We have now, Pamplemousse.' The Director looked him straight in the eye. 'All the resources of *Le Guide* will be at your disposal. Money will be no object. You may name your own fee.'

'It is not a question of money, *Monsieur* . . . '

'Good, Aristide. Then I will not embarrass you by raising the subject ever again. I knew I could count on your loyalty. It is only a temporary appointment, of course. Once we have surmounted the present problem we shall take steps to regularise the situation, but time is not on our side.'

Monsieur Pamplemousse stared at his chief. There were times when his ability to take things for granted and ride roughshod over people's sensibilities was positively beyond belief. It would have been nice to have had the matter raised just once more; an opportunity to protest a trifle less vehemently on the subject of his remuneration would not have come amiss. But the moment was lost forever. Perhaps reading his thoughts, the Director turned on his heels and went back inside.

Almost as though it were in sympathy, the sun disappeared again. Monsieur Pamplemousse took one last look over the parapet. Paris suddenly seemed to have grown in size.

What was the population of the greater area of the city at the last count? Something over ten million people. And he would be looking for perhaps just one person in all that number – it was hard to picture a whole group waging a vendetta against *Le Guide*.

Despite his protestations, his mind was already racing with thoughts and ideas. The Director was right. Speed and secrecy were both of paramount importance. If the news did leak out they would be done for. He must get on to Glandier straight away – together with anyone else who might have seen the print-out – and impress that fact on them.

Next, he would need to know who'd had access to the computer. Was it remotely possible for it to have been an outside job? If it wasn't, then it would make his task that much easier. If it was, then he hardly knew where to start. One thing was certain: he would need to take a crash course to end all crash courses on the subject before he could even begin to ask the right questions, let alone understand the answers.

'Well, Aristide?' The Director looked up from his desk as Monsieur Pamplemousse entered the room.

'Tell me about the computer, *Monsieur*.'

'Ah, yes, the computer.' A slightly glazed expression entered the Director's eyes. 'I have to confess that once the decision was made to commit *Le Guide* to what I believe are known as "*les disques*", a term which put me in mind of a *salle de danse* when I first heard it used, and once a suitable model had been chosen – if I remember correctly, it is a Poulanc DB23, the 457 version, if that means anything to you – I left the matter very much in the hands of the experts.'

'Do you know what language it speaks, *Monsieur*?' Grabbing at straws, Monsieur Pamplemousse tried to make it sound as though he knew what he was talking about.

The Director gave a snort. 'An alien language, Pamplemousse. One which is totally beyond my comprehension. It is, I believe, largely a question of "bytes" and "rams", neither of which are terms I even remotely begin to understand, nor do I wish to. Life is complicated enough as it is without such esoteric subdivisions.'

'I was really thinking of security, *Monsieur*. How, *par exemple*, could the computer have been made to produce a print-out which is so full of inaccuracies? At this moment it isn't so much a matter of knowing who did it, but rather *how* it was done. If we know the answer to the last question it may provide us with an answer to the first.'

'Ah, there you have me, Pamplemousse. There you have me. At my insistence security is as perfect as what I believe they somewhat prosaically call "the state of the art" can make it.'

'With respect, *Monsieur*, security is usually only as good as the people who operate it.'

'True, Pamplemousse, true. However, in this case you are dealing with a situation where information relating to the new issue of *Le Guide* can only be accessed provided the correct code-word is used. A code-word which is changed on a daily basis and is known to but two people, myself included.'

'And the other person, *Monsieur*? May I know who it is?'

'It is Madame Grante. In the fullness of time we plan to extend the range of the machine to include all our accounting procedures. Naturally this will take time, but . . . '

'How did she take to the thought of being computerised, *Monsieur*?'

The Director raised his hands. 'Understandably, she was not wildly enthusiastic at first. People, particularly of Madame Grante's age and disposition, are resistant to change. But gradually she came round to seeing our point of view – particularly when she began to realise the very positive advantages it would have. Information which would normally take her weeks to collate will be at her fingertips by the mere pressing of a button. P39s will no longer pile up in her pending tray. It was largely because I needed her goodwill that I brought her into the project at an early stage rather than confront her with it later as a *fait accompli*. The interesting thing is that once she accepted the idea she seemed to take to it like a *canard* to water. She has been working overtime every night for the last few months, mastering the new techniques. I shudder to think what the wages bill would have been otherwise. It would not be too much to say that she has become a changed person; it has obviously been a challenge to her and she has gained a new lease of life. It was because of that I entrusted her with entering the names of all those who have qualified for Stock Pot status in this year's guide.'

'You will not object if I question her, *Monsieur*?'

The Director eyed him nervously. 'Of course not, Pamplemousse. As I said earlier, you have *carte blanche*. In fact,' he reached for a telephone, 'I will ask my secretary to have her come up straight away. It will be as well if she knows you have my full approval.'

Monsieur Pamplemousse waited patiently, listening to what appeared to be a somewhat one-sided conversation. His end of it was made up of a series of monosyllabic replies which grew steadily less assured with every passing moment. He suspected he knew the reason why. At long last the Director put the phone down. He looked worried.

'Apparently she didn't come to work today. She left early yesterday afternoon in order to visit the hairdresser and hasn't been seen or heard of since.'

'Perhaps she wanted to look her best for today's ceremony, *Monsieur*. Something may have happened since then.'

'That is true.' The Director didn't look entirely convinced. 'However, it doesn't explain why she has not been in touch. It is most unlike her.'

They both sat in silence for a moment or two.

'What are you thinking, Pamplemousse?'

'I was thinking I would still like to see her, *Monsieur*.'

'I meant, what are you *really* thinking? You surely don't suspect anything untoward on her part. Madame Grante may have her faults, but I would stake my life on her integrity.'

Monsieur Pamplemousse spread his hands out, palms uppermost. 'At this stage, *Monsieur*, I suspect nothing and no one. I have an open mind. Nevertheless, given the circumstances, it does seem strange that she should be absent today of all days.'

If he'd given voice to his innermost thoughts it wasn't so much the possibility of Madame Grante doing anything untoward – he agreed with the Director, she was a model of rectitude – rather that something untoward might have happened to her. An accident on the way home from the office, a fall; they were just two possibilities. He didn't dare mention a third that had occurred to him. Instead, he chose another one at random.

'You say she is a changed woman, *Monsieur*. Perhaps it is not the computer at all. Perhaps she has a lover.'

The Director eyed him dubiously. 'Is that possible, Pamplemousse? A flight of fancy, surely?'

'He could be a masochist, *Monsieur*. During my time in the force I met many such men. Men who like nothing better than to be constantly punished.'

The Director fell silent for a moment, lost in thought. 'I must admit to having noticed that she has also changed her mode of dress of late. Her skirts have definitely been getting shorter and she has started wearing make-up.'

'All women are the victims of fashion, *Monsieur*. Madame Pamplemousse is always grumbling because the fashions are not what she wants.'

'My secretary also tells me Madame Grante was heard singing a selection from "Bless the Bride" recently. Apparently it was all round the office.'

Monsieur Pamplemousse began to wish he hadn't brought up the subject. It had only been meant as a joke. A rather poor one at that.

'I think, before I do anything else, *Monsieur*, I should go and see her. If you could let me have her address.'

The Director picked up his telephone again. 'I will ask my secretary. I know it is somewhere on the right bank.' He had the grace to look slightly shame-faced. 'I should know, of course.'

It was, in fact, typical of Madame Grante that the Director didn't know. Monsieur Pamplemousse had no idea either. Occasionally on his way to the office by *autobus* he'd seen her coming along the Rue Saint-Dominique, but he'd always immediately looked the other way rather than risk having to walk to the office with her. Conversation with Madame Grante wasn't the easiest thing in the world, especially first thing in the morning. It was usually confined to mundane matters like expenses. Anything else was likely to be frowned on. Enquiries into her personal life were treated with suspicion, almost like attempted rape.

'*Merci.*' The Director reached for his pad, jotted down a number, then tore off the top sheet. He turned to Monsieur Pamplemousse. 'She has an apartment in the Rue des Renaudes in the seventeenth *arrondissement*.'

Monsieur Pamplemousse rose to his feet. 'I will go straight

away, *Monsieur.*' He doubted if he would learn much more from Madame Grante than he had from the Director, but at least she would have a working knowledge of the computer. Anyway it was a case of first things first and he suddenly wanted to be on the move.

The Director looked less than enthusiastic. 'You could be wasting your time, Pamplemousse. Apparently Véronique – who, by the way, is the only other person who knows what has happened – has tried more than once to telephone her, but each time there has been no reply.'

'I have to begin somewhere, *Monsieur.*'

The Director gave a sigh. 'Ah, well, if you must you must. But remember, we have less than a week to go before publication. Each and every hour of the day is precious. In the meantime, while you are gone I shall put a team of girls from the typing pool to work on recompiling *Le Guide.* They will be fighting a losing battle, I fear, but it will be something to fall back on if need be. I shall also tighten security. The whole building will be put on *alerte rouge.* As from tomorrow no one will be allowed in or out without production of a pass and positive means of identification.'

'That sounds sensible.' Monsieur Pamplemousse couldn't but feel that it was a case of locking the stable door after the horse had bolted. He looked at the Director speculatively. Mention of there being less than a week to go before publication had reminded him of Doucette's comment during *petit déjeuner* when she had read the item in the *journal.* He wondered if the Director had noticed the misprint too. Correction: for the first time he found himself wondering if it really had been a misprint, or whether the wrong date had some deeper significance. He decided not to mention the matter, at least for the time being. The Director had enough worries on his mind.

Instead, he excused himself and was about to make his way into the outer office when the Director called him back.

'Pamplemousse, I shall be grateful if you would remove that ridiculous object from Pommes Frites' collar. I appreciate the thought, but I scarcely need a walking reminder of how black the situation is.'

'Of course, *Monsieur*.' The truth of the matter was that what with one thing and another Monsieur Pamplemousse had totally forgotten Pommes Frites had also gone into mourning.

Anticipating his wishes, the Director's secretary had a map of Paris open on her desk. 'Madame Grante's apartment is near the Place des Ternes. Would you like me to call a taxi?'

Monsieur Pamplemousse shook his head. 'I will find my own way there.' He consulted another map in his diary. Travelling by Métro would involve changing trains twice, a tedious business in the rush hour. Madame Grante probably only did it on rainy days. More than likely she normally caught the 92 *autobus* in the Avenue Bosquet and got off in the Avenue Niel. It would be nice to do the same; a way of easing himself gradually into her way of life.

He glanced down. Taking his friend and mentor along as well would be out of the question. Rules and regulations forbade it. There was no way he could squeeze Pommes Frites into a travelling box no larger than 21cm by 10cm, still less carry it if he did. Once upon a time he could have travelled like any other normal passenger, but nowadays there was no way he would be allowed on board. Any argument and the driver would reach for the telephone beside his left ear and call headquarters. Perhaps they should take their chance on the Métro after all and hope they didn't encounter one of the roving bands of ticket Inspectors. Either that or accept the offer of a taxi, but what he wanted most at that moment was space, and time to think.

'*Permettez-moi?*' He picked up the telephone and dialled an outside number.

His call was answered almost immediately.

'Jacques, Aristide here . . . ' The first few questions confirmed the Director's fears. Computer crime was an area where the rapid advance in technology far outstripped the means of combating it, at least as far as the police were concerned. Help was available but it wouldn't be immediate – it was mainly left to the Fraud Squad and they were understaffed and overworked. In any case it was a situation where the law itself was even further behind. Obtaining a conviction in a case involving computer crime was fraught with difficulties. Attempting it was often a waste of time and manpower.

Monsieur Pamplemousse listened patiently. Although it wasn't entirely unexpected, it wasn't exactly what he wanted to hear either. When he mentioned the time scale there was a hollow laugh.

'OK. Have you any other ideas then?'

'*Un moment.*' There was a pause while names were thrown around. Eventually Jacques came back to him. 'I'm told there is someone in Passy . . . name of Borel.'

'Could you make an appointment for me?'

'When?'

'This evening if possible.' He looked at his watch. It showed 16.30. 'Say, 18.30-19.00 hrs. Before *dîner*. Tell them it is urgent.'

'*D'accord.* I'll hold on.' While he was waiting Monsieur Pamplemousse glanced at the map on the desk. The Rue des Renaudes wasn't that far. Three-quarters of an hour at the most. The walk would do them both good.

'*Merci. Vous êtes un copain.*' He put the receiver down at long last. He may have drawn a blank with help from his old department in the *Sûreté*, but at least the call had gained him an appointment with a 'consultant' who could be trusted. It was better than nothing.

He dialled his home number.

'Couscous. I fear I shall be home late.

'No. Something has come up. I am needed here . . .

' . . . it is not possible to say at present.

'Why don't you go and stay with Agathe?

'Good. I will see you when I see you.

'*Au revoir, chérie.* Take care.'

He replaced the receiver. Doucette had sounded resigned. How many times had they had the same conversation in his days with the *Sûreté*? He had lost count. Her sister in Melun had always been the chief beneficiary of his enforced

38

absences.

'If you are taking Pommes Frites with you,' said
Véronique, 'I should make sure he wipes his paws before he
goes in. You know what Madame Grante is like.'

'*Poof!*' Monsieur Pamplemousse blew her a kiss. She
caught it expertly and put it in a desk drawer for safe keeping.
'Call me if you have any news or if you need anything.'

He paused outside the door, then headed, not towards the
main lift, but to a smaller one at the far end of the corridor.
He had one more call to make before he left the building.

Madame Grante's secretary was new, which wasn't unduly
surprising. Madame Grante got through secretaries rather
quicker than most people got through writing out their expenses sheets. It would be interesting to see if the new computer stayed the course. Perhaps the current trouble was a
forewarning of things to come, the electronic equivalent of a
cry for help.

Madame Grante's secretary was not only new, she was less
than helpful. Monsieur Pamplemousse had the feeling that the
boss's absence was the best thing that had happened to the
Accounts Department that week.

No, she had no idea why Madame Grante hadn't turned
up for work. Madame Grante didn't confide in her. Sniff.

No, she hadn't noticed anything different about the way
Madame Grante had been behaving. She hadn't been working
at *Le Guide* long enough to know. Sniff. Sniff.

She didn't actually say that she wouldn't be staying long
enough to find out, but the underlying message was there,
loud and clear.

Monsieur Pamplemousse took his leave. On the way down
the corridor he tried the door of the new computer room. It
was locked. He had been in there once – soon after it had
been installed. At the time he had found it somewhat disap-
pointing: windowless, air-conditioned and antiseptic. Even
the sheer lack of size of the machine itself, standing in splen-
did isolation in the centre of the floor, had been a bit of a
disappointment. Given the fact that one way and another it
was destined to control all their working lives he would have

preferred something larger, something with more wires and with glass panels he could look through in order to see what was going on inside. It was so neat and unassuming it was almost as sinister as the clicks and grunts it emitted randomly from time to time.

Apart from the computer and its associated equipment – keyboards, visual display units, and some racks containing storage disks and other items, there had, in fact, been surprisingly little to see. All the same, he would have liked to have gone inside the room again, if only to refresh his memory.

Acting on an impulse he went back to Madame Grante's department. The girl was on the telephone and she didn't look overpleased to see him.

'Do you have the key to the computer room?'

She shook her head, then put her hand over the mouthpiece. 'You could try looking in Madame Grante's desk if you like.' She nodded towards an open door leading to the inner sanctum. 'She keeps a few spare keys there. If it's around at all it will be in the top drawer on the right. Otherwise they're probably all in her handbag.'

Conscious that he was being watched, Monsieur Pamplemousse tried the desk drawer. It was locked. He pulled at the others one by one, instinctively preparing himself to jump back should Madame Grante happen to appear unexpectedly. They were all locked. He was tempted to try his own keys on them, but he wasn't sure how the girl would take it.

There was a computer terminal near by. The keyboard and screen were both neatly concealed beneath grey plastic covers. He tried the one drawer below the table top. That, too, was locked.

He thanked the girl and left. As he closed the door behind him he heard her voice. 'Sorry about that. Now, about tonight . . . '

Pommes Frites, glad to be out in the fresh air again, set a brisk pace and they reached the Pont de l'Alma in under ten minutes. A heavily laden barge pushing two others swept past, helped on its way by the fast-moving current. He caught a

glimpse of the skipper concentrating on the view ahead before
it disappeared under one of the arches. The *quais* which a few
weeks before had been under water were now almost clear.
Traffic was on the move again on the through-roads and the
Vedettes moored further upstream were floodlit. He leaned
over the parapet and looked down at the statue of the *zouave*
– the French Algerian soldier who for generations had helped
passing Parisians gauge the height of the Seine. His boots
were now clear of the muddied waters. Bits of debris stuck to
the plinth.

There was no doubt in his mind that despite all its many
benefits the computer could also be a disruptive influence.
For better or for worse it upset the balance of things. Get on
the wrong side of one and you were in trouble. The thought
of having his P39s committed to a plastic *disque*, available for
instant analysis and comparison with previous entries, was
hard to contemplate.

Much as one grumbled about having to indulge in arguments with Madame Grante on the subject of expenses, there
was no denying the pleasure of an occasional battle won – it
more than made up for all the lost ones. It wouldn't be the
same thing at all with a computer.

The Inspector who used his car for a Saturday shopping
trip would feel very hard done by if on Monday morning the
computer deleted the mileage from his work sheet.

On the other hand, there was no good fighting it. It was
here to stay. Some years before, if they had chosen to do so,
he and Doucette could have had one of the Minitel terminals
France Télécom distributed free on request to all their subscribers. Originally intended to replace the telephone directory, they were now used for all manner of things. Banks, the
Stock Exchange, purveyors of junk mail. If you were doing a
personalised mail-shot to local plumbers, it was possible to
select all the men in a town of your choice whose first name
was Jean. On the other side of the coin, it was said that a
growing number of subscribers dialled 36 15 in order to work
out their erotic fantasies via *messageries roses*. Others used the
system to order their groceries. He couldn't picture Doucette

doing her shopping that way. The chief beneficiaries were Télécom, who were making a fortune out of the phone calls, and the program makers.

From the Pont de l'Alma to the Etoile took Monsieur Pamplemousse and Pommes Frites fifteen minutes. From the Etoile down the Avenue de Wagram less than another ten – he'd forgotten how much of a downhill slope there was. He hadn't been far out in his calculations. The market in the Rue Poncelet was alive and bustling. He used to shop there at one time and still occasionally bought the Christmas ham in Aux Fermes d'Auvergne. No doubt it was where Madame Grante did all her food shopping; there would be no point in going further afield.

Madame Grante's apartment was in an anonymous row of stone-clad seven-floored buildings whose uniformly vertical façades reflected the strict rules first laid down by Baron Haussmann. The architect's name was engraved in a stone high up on the wall alongside a date – 1906.

The large wooden door – normally opened by a key-operated lock – was standing ajar. On the wall just inside there was an array of entryphone buttons. He ran his finger down the list of names. Madame Grante's apartment was on the fourth floor. He pressed a button opposite her name and waited. On the other side of a glass-panelled door he could see an antiquated lift, hardly big enough for more than two people at a time.

While he was waiting, a man came in from the street, checked his mail in a row of boxes on the opposite wall, then opened the inner door. He looked at them enquiringly. The combination of Monsieur Pamplemousse's dark suit and Pommes Frites' august presence must have lent an air of respectability, for he stood to one side and held the door open for them.

'*Monsieur . . .*'

'*Merci, Monsieur.*' Monsieur Pamplemousse took advantage of the offer. He had a feeling he wasn't about to get anywhere with the entryphone.

On the grounds that the exercise would do him good, he

made for the stairs. It saved concocting a story. Half-way up he passed a room where someone was playing a saxophone. He was no Charlie Parker.

Madame Grante's apartment was one of two which ran the width of the building. He rang the bell and waited, but again there was no reply and he was about to leave when he heard a strange scuffling noise. Putting his ear to the door Monsieur Pamplemousse thought he detected the sound of a movement on the other side – the rustle of a gown, perhaps; it was hard to place. It was followed by what sounded like a voice in the distance, but it was impossible to make out the words. He tried pressing the bell-push a second time – the response was loud and clear – but the sound died away to nothing.

Taking out his notepad and pen, he scribbled a brief message saying he had called and asking Madame Grante to contact the office as soon as possible. Tearing the sheet of paper from its pad, he bent down and tried to slip it through the gap between the bottom of the door and the floor. It met with resistance half-way through, probably from a mat, leaving a small corner protruding into the corridor.

He crouched down on his hands and knees in an attempt to push the paper through even further, and as he did so he heard the rustling noise again, only louder this time. A moment later there was a tug and the paper was wrenched from his fingers. Pommes Frites made a dive, but he wasn't quick enough.

Monsieur Pamplemousse jumped guiltily to his feet and waited for the door to open, but he waited in vain. Once again total silence reigned. He gave a shrug. Clearly, for reasons best known to herself, Madame Grante was not at home to callers. He didn't feel inclined to press the matter, but it was hardly a good start to the evening.

On his way out of the building, he checked her mailbox. Through the clear plastic door he could see a small pile of letters – mostly circulars. Either she hadn't bothered to empty it that day, or there was some other reason for their having been left. Whatever the cause, Monsieur Pamplemousse was left with a vague sense of unease.

As they left the building he crossed over to the other side of the street and glanced up towards the fourth floor, but the windows were covered by net curtains and there was no sign of movement.

Retracing his steps in the direction of the Etoile, he called in at a little bar near the Avenue Niel and ordered a *Cardinal*. The Cassis, its freshness preserved in a refrigerator beneath the counter, was a *Double Crème* from Ropiteau Frères, rich and intensely fruity, the Beaujolais of Juliénas, purple and deliciously young; the bittersweet mixture suited his current mood. He brooded over it for a moment or two. It was good to be getting his teeth into something new, but on the other hand he wished it wasn't quite so close to home. After the first glass he began to feel better. After the second, he felt ready for the fray.

He looked at his watch. It was 17.45; time he met Monsieur Borel, the computer expert.

3

THE RIGHT CONNECTIONS

The address Monsieur Pamplemousse had been given turned
out to be a smart apartment block off the Rue Raynouard in
the sixteenth *arrondissement*. It was as different to Madame
Grante's as it was possible to imagine. As he approached the
entrance, plate-glass doors parted in the middle, opening
onto an entrance hall which could have housed his own
apartment several times over. He decided that if the architect
– whose name was engraved on a bronze plaque let into the
floor – had shares in the company who'd supplied the marble,
he must have done extremely well out of the deal.

To one side of the hall there was a large desk with a bank of
closed-circuit television monitors. Behind it sat a poker-faced
man in uniform. It was hard to tell what he was thinking, if
indeed he thought anything at all. The man gazed non-
committally at Pommes Frites while he telephoned the news
of their arrival. In return Pommes Frites gave as good as he
got.

There were four lifts – two either side of a rock-garden full
of artificial foliage which was the centre piece of a wide
passageway leading off from the rear of the hall. Monsieur
Pamplemousse took the first lift to arrive and pressed a button for the tenth floor. As the doors closed he became aware
of a camera lens high up in one corner. He turned his back on
it. A few moments later, just as imperceptibly as it had
started, the lift came to rest again. As the doors opened he
found himself entering a small vestibule. The dark brown
carpet was thick underfoot; pictures on the walls reflected
bulk-buying rather than any artistic aspirations. They were

probably the same on every floor. He wondered if the architect had shares in that company too. He pressed a bell-push on the door facing him and waited.

Even before it opened he knew exactly what Monsieur Borel would look like. He would be casually dressed, bearded – probably wearing open-toed sandals. If he wore socks they would be brightly coloured. He would have steel-rimmed spectacles and he would blink a lot as a result of having spent most of his life glued to video screens. His forehead would be domed, his receding hair would need cutting, and he would be so intelligent he would most likely be unable to understand the few simple questions Monsieur Pamplemousse wished to ask. In his spare time he probably compiled handbooks for Eastern manufacturers of electronic equipment, translating them into a language which neither they nor their customers would understand. His large black watch would have an illuminated dial showing the time and date at any given moment in all continents of the world – even if he happened to be under water when he wanted to know. It would probably emit 'pings' at set intervals.

He was wrong on all nine counts – ten if you included the fact that it wasn't Monsieur Borel; it was Mademoiselle, and Mademoiselle Martine Borel was thirtyish, slim, well groomed, expensively dressed, cool and efficient. *Soignée* perhaps rather than chic. Her make-up was impeccably understated, and her glasses were large and round, with black frames to match her hair. Just to confuse the issue, she wore a Mickey Mouse watch on her left wrist. The flicker of surprise must have shown on his face.

'They obviously didn't tell you?'

From the way she said it and from the amused look in her eyes Monsieur Pamplemousse guessed it wasn't the first time it had happened. He covered his embarrassment by removing his hat and gesturing towards Pommes Frites.

'I hope you have no objection.'

'On the contrary. Besides, I was told you might be accompanied.'

'His name is Pommes Frites. He goes everywhere with

me.'

'So I believe.'

She bent down to pat Pommes Frites, then took Monsieur Pamplemousse's hat from him and placed it on a shelf in a cupboard. She was wearing a slim gold bangle on her right wrist, but no rings. He spotted a Louis Vuitton bag on the floor and wondered if it was real or a fake. It was hard to tell these days; the *Musée de la Contrefaçon* was full of examples of the latter. If it was the former, the Director might find himself in for a sizeable bill.

As Mademoiselle Borel turned to lead the way into a large open-plan living-room he noticed she had a few grey hairs. Perhaps she was older than she looked.

From the wide picture-windows he could see across the rooftops of Paris towards the Eiffel Tower. The roads on either side of the Seine were already full of evening traffic. He glanced around the room. One wall was almost entirely covered by shelves. Most of the shelves were filled with books, interspersed with items of bric-à-brac. The remaining walls had a scattering of paintings – mostly modern. There were several pieces of modern sculpture dotted around, lit by equally modern lamps. There was also a faint, but delicious smell of something cooking. Pommes Frites licked his lips in pleasurable anticipation as he settled himself down on a rug in the centre of the room, eyeing his surroundings with evident approval.

On a low glass-topped table between two black leather armchairs there was a tray on which stood two tall glasses of white wine and a bottle in an ice bucket. There was also a bowl of black olives and a plate of *amuse-gueule* in the shape of tiny tartlets. Beside the tray lay a slim black folder.

'Please help yourself.' Mademoiselle Borel crossed the room, closed a door leading to the kitchen, then returned carrying a bowl of water which she placed on the floor in front of Pommes Frites. Settling herself comfortably in one of the chairs, she draped one leg elegantly over the other, then pointed to the folder. 'My c.v.'

'*Merci.*' Monsieur Pamplemousse opened it as he took the

other chair. Normally he might not have bothered, accepting the recommendation he'd been given on trust, but he was intrigued.

Born in Lyon, the only daughter of a shop-keeping family, Martine Borel had been educated first in the city itself where she had gained her *baccalauréat*, then at the *élite* Grenoble Technical University. After that had come a spell at MIT in Boston, followed by a job in California's Silicon Valley; then back to France and Honeywell-Bull before going it alone as a consultant. She had two books to her credit; one on computer security, the other with a more philosophic sounding title. She hadn't always been Mademoiselle. Somewhere along the line there had been a marriage and a divorce, so she hadn't emerged from it all entirely unscathed. Perhaps it accounted for the grey hairs.

The tartlets were warm and freshly made. They were filled with a beaten mixture of tunny fish, anchovies, chopped gherkin and mayonnaise, with a few capers to taste.

The wine was cold and unfamiliar; a total contrast to his *Cardinal*. He tried hard to place it. He could taste all kinds of fruits: peaches, plums, apples, a hint of lemon. It was a very elegant wine.

She caught him glancing at the label on the bottle as she refilled his glass.

'It is a Château Bouchamie Carneros.'

He was none the wiser.

'It is a Chardonnay from California.'

'Ah, California.'

She caught the nuance in his voice and was about to say something.

'It is very good,' he added hastily. 'In fact, it is more than very good. It is excellent.'

'One must not be chauvinistic. The Americans have a lot to learn about wine, but they are quick and dedicated. In a very short space of time they have also taught us many things – even though in the beginning we were reluctant to admit the possibility.'

He put down the file. It was time to change the subject.

'You have led a very full life.'

'Do I get the job?' Again there was a hint of amusement in the eyes. She was very sure of herself.

'If you can call it that. I am in need of advice.'

'What can I do to help? I was told only that you wish to know about computers.'

'Starting from the beginning. *Par exemple*, I know that "hardware" refers to the basic machinery you can actually touch, and that "software" refers to the programs which make it work, but beyond that . . . ' He spread out his hands. 'I am lost.'

She made a face. 'It is a large order.'

'It is a large problem and there is not much time.'

'I see. Well, assuming that all external connections are correct . . . '

Monsieur Pamplemousse's pride was stung. 'I do know a little more than that.'

'Perhaps. But is one of the most useful phrases I was ever taught. I still say it to myself whenever I have a problem. How many times have you seen people take an iron or an electric toaster to be repaired and it turns out not to have been switched on at the wall – or even plugged in? You shouldn't take it too literally. It applies to life as well as to computers.'

Monsieur Pamplemousse accepted the reproof. 'Let us assume all external connections are correct.'

'You are a brave man. Tell me, after the hall porter had announced you, what did you do?'

'I came up to your floor.'

'Exactly. And how did you reach it?'

'I pressed the button for the lift. It arrived. I got in. Then I pressed another button for the tenth floor . . . '

'And did you ask yourself why all these things happened?'

'No.'

'Of course not. To use a lift it is not necessary to know how it works. So why should you know how a computer works? It is usually sufficient that it does.'

'Suppose I wished to arrange matters so that when the lift reached the tenth floor it didn't stop but went on to the twelfth.'

'Ah, *then* you would need to know about lifts. You would also need to know something about aerodynamics – for the moment when it went through the roof. There are only ten floors.'

Touché! He felt himself warming towards her. 'Fortunately in my case lifts do not come into it. I only wish to know how someone might "arrange matters" with a computer. With that end in view, I feel it would be nice to know how they work.'

She nodded. 'They are like many other complicated things – taking a photograph, for example, or television – once they are broken down into their basic elements they are really very simple.

'Think of a long corridor with door after door after door. If all the doors are open you can walk straight through, but if just one of those doors is locked, then you can't. Take that a stage further. Supposing at each door there is a man who asks you a simple question to which the answer is either "TRUE" or "FALSE". If the answer is "TRUE" you can go through. If it is "FALSE" then you are out of the game. A computer works on much the same principle. It is a series of doors.

'Think, too, of the fact that the latest IBM door can be opened and closed some thirty billion times a second.'

'Even computers occasionally come up with wrong answers. They stop people going through doors when they shouldn't, or vice versa.'

'Computers very rarely come up with the wrong answer.' For the first time there was a hint of irritation in her voice. 'If they do – if for some reason they develop a fault – then the answer is usually so wildly wrong the fact should be obvious to anyone who has half an inkling of what the right one should be. People often ask computers the wrong question, then blame it when they don't like what it tells them. It is very easy to blame something you don't understand. If computers have a fault it is that they have spawned a whole society which can't add up because it has no need to, and isn't prepared to accept responsibility for its own mistakes.'

Monsieur Pamplemousse pondered the matter for a moment or two while more wine was poured. The truth of the matter was they were playing with each other. He decided the first move was up to him. He would come clean. Instinctively he trusted her. Anyone who liked wine and had such delicious smells coming from her kitchen had to be trusted. He gave the woman a brief run-down of all that had happened to date.

'That is terrible!'

'For *Le Guide* it is worse than terrible. It could be disastrous.'

'One thing is very certain. If the entries are wrong but make sense, then it is not a mistake on the part of the computer. It has to be a deliberate act on the part of someone else.'

'Exactly.'

'For what purpose? Presumably it is not fraud. I mean, no money is involved?'

'We may not be concerned with money directly – but indirectly a great deal is involved. Over one million copies of *Le Guide* are sold each year at a published price of one hundred and fifty francs per copy. That is a lot of money.'

'And no royalties to pay!'

'No royalties to pay.'

'But that would point to a rival and from all you say that seems very unlikely.'

'I cannot picture it.'

'So if we rule that out, and if it isn't to do with the shifting of money, then how about revenge?'

'Revenge? That is a possibility, I suppose, although I can't think of a reason. Be that as it may, it is my brief to find out who is responsible, and to do that it would be helpful to find out how it could have been done.'

She thought for a moment or two. 'There are two possibilities. Either it was done from outside the building, or it was done by someone inside. I have to tell you here and now that the second is the more likely of the two. Most computer break-ins are made by members of staff. Do you know what kind of computer it is? What make?'

'It is – ' Monsieur Pamplemousse took out his notebook. 'It is a Poulanc DB23, 450 series. What is known as a main-frame computer I believe.'

She looked impressed. 'Nothing but the best! It has a memory of over sixty-four million bytes. They've developed a new type of laser-operated head. It gives data storage of over 500 million characters on *disque*, would you believe?'

Monsieur Pamplemousse tried his best to look fascinated. Words like "byte" were still as much like Greek to him as they were to the Director.

'So you probably have a number of work stations dotted about the building?' He realised she was still talking.

'There are a good many, and there are network sockets everywhere for when we need to expand.'

Mademoiselle Borel gave a shrug as if to say there is your answer. 'Are the satellites live or dumb?'

'Meaning?'

'Do they operate through the mainframe computer, or are they PCs – desk-top computers – capable of operating inde-pendently? In other words, would it be possible to feed a program into the main computer from one of them?'

Monsieur Pamplemousse had to confess he didn't know.

'There is a whole history of computers being broken into from outside, but it usually requires time, a good deal of skill and an element of luck. In 1983 a nineteen-year-old student caused consternation in high places by breaking into the Pentagon computer. Messages have been left on the NASA Space Agency computer. In England the Duke of Edin-burgh's personal electronic mail was penetrated on Prestel. Mostly it is done by "hackers" for the sheer hell of it. They see it as a challenge – like climbing Mount Everest.'

'So it is possible?'

'Let us just say that nothing is impossible. Whole books have been written about computer fraud. As you saw, I have had one published myself. It has simply become more diffi-cult, that is all. Manufacturers try to keep one pace ahead. But it is certainly not impossible.'

'Tell me more.'

'To enter a system from the outside you need to go in through the "front door", as it were. For that, all you require is a home computer and a "modem" to connect it to the public telephone. How many people know that it exists?'

'A good many, I imagine. There is nothing secret about the installation – only the contents. It has been mentioned more than once in the trade *journaux*. You could say it is an "open secret".'

'Does *Le Guide* provide a service for outside customers?'

'An information service will be available. Two, in fact. One for members of the public via France Télécom system, and another for accredited members of various trade organisations. Information will be available on payment of a subscription. It will also have the capability of being accessed by members of staff feeding in information while on their travels. Ultimately all Inspectors will have their own modems.' He was beginning to pick up the jargon.

'So in one respect you have already provided a good many people with a key to the front door?'

Monsieur Pamplemousse nodded gloomily. His task seemed to be getting more complex by the minute.

'You must also bear in mind that a newly installed computer is at its most vulnerable. A computer which has been in use for some years will have had all its bugs ironed out; a new one may have many problems. Who supplied the software – the part that operates it?'

'I believe it was bought in from an outside firm and modified to our requirements.'

'There have been cases of programs being set up to go wrong on a certain date. Some software manufacturers look on it as a form of insurance against bills not being paid, or contracts not being renewed. It is not impossible for someone to have programmed the computer to sabotage *Le Guide* on a certain date right from the start.'

Once again the questions of dates seemed to have cropped up. There was an underlying feeling of everything having been pre-planned which bothered him.

'What about security?'

'*Monsieur le Directeur* has always been very security conscious,' said Monsieur Pamplemousse, glad to be on firmer ground at long last. 'As far as the physical side is concerned, no one other than staff is ever allowed inside the building without first signing the visitors' book. Members of the public are allowed entry in order to visit the shop and a reference library, but while they are there they have to wear an adhesive badge. They are then required to sign the book again on leaving.'

'How about the badge? Is it handed in?'

'Of course. Visitors aren't allowed out of the building otherwise.'

'Good. That doesn't always happen. How about the computer room itself?'

'It is kept locked.'

'Presumably cleaners go in from time to time. Some people need to have access for other reasons. Computers need servicing. So do things like air-conditioning and sprinkler systems. It is often a case of no one noticing the *facteur* when he delivers the letters. Are references always taken up when people apply for a job?'

'I imagine so.'

'Most firms don't. Will you be checking mine?'

Monsieur Pamplemousse was tempted to say 'that is different', but he knew that it wasn't. He also couldn't help reflecting on the ease with which the girl in Madame Grante's office had offered him the key to the computer room. She had been too anxious to get back to her boyfriend to worry overmuch about security. Admittedly he had drawn a blank, but he might have found it. He wondered if her credentials had been checked. Knowing Madame Grante, he was sure they would have been.

'A new computer is always a disruptive influence. People see it as a threat to old established ways of doing their job. Also, you mustn't lose sight of it having been done by someone – or a group of people – with a grudge.'

'Someone with a grudge against *Le Guide*?' It was hard to imagine.

'I agree, but it does to some extent represent the privileged. Also, such groups see any computer as a menace to society. It is their vowed intention to challenge anyone or anything connected with them. In France they go under the name of the *Comité de Libération ou de Détournement des Ordinateurs*. CLODO for short. They have been responsible for a number of attacks – mostly against big companies in the Toulouse area.'

'*Clodo* is also the slang word for a tramp.'

She shrugged. 'Granted. But even I have to admit they have a point. For the first time it has become possible to encapsulate a man's whole life – both the good and the bad – on a tiny part of a single *disquette*. If we are not very careful, "Big Brother" could soon be watching over us, and computers are totally lacking in morals. It is not the aims of CLODO one disagrees with so much as their methods.

'Besides, they are much more likely to plant what is called a Logic Bomb – a program which is timed to go off at some predetermined date and cause irreparable damage. They are out to destroy – not to play games. Either that, or what is known as a "virus", a device which gradually eats away at the information. From all you have told me, neither seems likely.'

'But if it was an outside job?' he persisted. 'Assuming someone entered through the "front door" as you call it, how did they get any further? How did they enter the area which contains the contents of the new edition of *Le Guide*? For that it is necessary to use a password. One which is changed every day and is known to only two people.'

'What else?'

'That is not enough?'

'It is possible to place too much reliance on using a password. To use the "door" analogy once again, it is like having only one lock on the entrance but changing it every day. Sometimes it might be better to have two locks and only change them occasionally. If someone wishes to open a safe door and they don't know the combination, what do they do?'

'It depends. They can either go through all the possible combinations – which in most cases is an almost insurmountable problem because of the time factor. If they are very expert they might have listening apparatus, but that kind of thing usually only happens in films. They can blow it open – but that, too, has its problems. If it is a very small safe they might even carry it away and open it at their leisure. Or, they can try and find out the combination by other means. What is known as lateral thinking.'

'Exactly. The one advantage in looking for the "combination lock" on a computer is that provided you program another computer correctly you can use it to do all the hard work for you, particularly if the password is short – five letters or less. You say only two people know what it is?'

Monsieur Pamplemousse nodded.

'And are you one of the two?'

'No.' It hadn't occurred to him to ask the Director for it. In many ways he would rather not know.

'That is a plus.' She quickly corrected herself. 'I mean it is a plus that it wasn't given to you automatically. Now I will give you a negative. You say the password is changed every day? Presumably it is a word and not a number?'

'I was told it was a word.'

'Numbers are often safer. If you take two very large prime numbers and multiply them together it can be almost unbreakable. I will give you an example: the date of the French Revolution and the date of Hitler's rise to power – 1789 and 1933 – two prime numbers. Multiply them together and you get what is known as a "prime product" – 3,458,137 – it would take even the most powerful computer in the world years to find it.'

Monsieur Pamplemousse helped himself to another tart. 'It sounds as though I shall need a course in higher mathematics as well as electronics if I am to take part in the battle of the computer.'

Mademoiselle Borel laughed. 'I'm sorry – I wasn't trying to blind you with science. Anyway, I'm glad you said "of" not "with". The computer is entirely neutral. It is neither on your side, nor against you.'

Monsieur Pamplemousse took the point. 'I must be grateful for small mercies. So what do you suggest?'

'I think for the time being we must assume it is a word or a combination of words which is changed every day. To put it another way, there are 365 new words or combinations of words to learn in a year and as many to forget. That immediately narrows the field. Quite likely they will all be related in some way. Taken from a directory, perhaps. In the case of *Le Guide*, the chances are that it will be some word related to food or to wine. It could be the name of a cheese. Is there an official list?'

'The bible of the cheese industry is Androuet's *Guide du Fromage*.'

'So they could start at the beginning. The first one listed would be for one day, the second for day two, and so on . . . Or it could be wine.'

'There is the 1855 classification for Bordeaux wines.'

'But that would only give sixty-three. Enough for two months.'

Monsieur Pamplemousse looked at her with renewed respect. He couldn't have come up with the exact number himself.

She poured the rest of the wine.

'We could always give it a try.'

'What . . . now?'

'There is no time like the present. When do the staff go home?'

'Most of them leave around five thirty or six o'clock. There is a round-the-clock service operated by a skeleton staff, but as far as I know there will be no one operating the computer.'

Mademoiselle Borel looked at her watch. 'Good. It is after six. That's when most hacking is done. Weekends are usually the peak time. It's surprising how even big firms leave their systems to fend for themselves at weekends. We will carry out a little test.'

Handing him his glass she stood up and led the way towards a door on the far side of the room. He followed, and to his surprise suddenly found himself entering a room full of equipment. He could have been in a mini version of Mission Control Houston for all most of it meant to him. Mademoiselle Borel ran through a series of switches. Warning lights came on. There was a faint hum of electronic machinery. Warning bleeps issued from all sides. Screens began to glow.

On the balcony there were two small dish aerials. Beyond them he could see across the river towards his own office. If he'd had his Leitz glasses with him he would probably have been able to see the Director's office. He was glad he couldn't. He had a momentary mental vision of the Director doing exactly the same thing in reverse and their eyes meeting.

Below lay the Rue Berton, the little lane which Honoré de Balzac used when he wanted to escape from his creditors while he was living at number 47, working through the night and keeping himself awake by drinking black coffee, a combination which eventually proved lethal. A little way up the hill there was a figure in dark blue uniform clutching a machine carbine. No doubt he was guarding the Turkish Embassy.

Mademoiselle Borel glanced round as he took a closer look at the aerials. 'They are the modern equivalent of phone tapping. The air is full of information – twenty-four hours a day – flying in all directions.'

She motioned towards a second chair as she seated herself in front of a console, inserted a *disquette* and began punching in a series of commands.

Almost at once he was aware of a change in the atmosphere. Gone was the laid-back Mademoiselle Borel who had received him. In her place was a highly dedicated and knowledgeable professional.

'The first thing to do is dial up the mainframe computer. Do you have the number?'

Monsieur Pamplemousse consulted his notebook again and gave it to her.

She typed it in. There was a pause, then a welcoming

BONJOUR appeared on a screen in front of them. It was followed by a request for identification.

'Any ideas?'

Monsieur Pamplemousse felt a momentary pang of guilt. It was almost as though he were breaking into his own house. Worse than that even. It felt like a betrayal of trust. 'You could try one of the other guides. Michelin, perhaps, or Gault-Millau. I'm sure they subscribe. Or any of the major *journaux*.'

'I will try *Le Monde*.'

She typed the words and they appeared on the screen.

'Which service do you require?' The reply was almost instantaneous.

She looked enquiringly at Monsieur Pamplemousse. He shrugged.

'I will ask for their HELP menu. If we are very lucky it may give the kind of vital information we need – like how to enter other areas. It has been known.'

A long list flashed on the screen. At the bottom were the words LE GUIDE.

'I don't believe it.' She selected the appropriate command on her keyboard. 'It can't be that easy.'

'MOT DE PASSE, S'IL VOUS PLAIT' appeared on the screen.

'I'll try thinking up a password at random and see what happens.'

After the third attempt the screen went blank. She made a grimace.

'It isn't as easy as it looks! The machine has been pro-grammed to cut off the call after the third attempt. It is a common safeguard. The problem now is that it has quite probably automatically logged in the time and date. Once can be a genuine mistake, or simply someone who is interested. A whole series of repeated attempts will arouse suspicion.'

'How would you get round that?'

'If you were able to access the security section you could delete the information it has logged.'

'And if you couldn't?'

She shrugged. 'There are always other ways. Speaking for

myself, I would put plan "B" into operation. I might arrange for someone to pose as a telephone engineer and insert a listening device where the lines enter the building. He could then pick up any messages via a receiver outside the building and feed it into a computer. Once you are in, there is often a device known as a "Zap Utility" which exists for all sorts of purposes – maintenance, writing of new applications. If you can enter that, the world is your oyster. You can edit away to your heart's content. Create new files . . . '

Monsieur Pamplemousse sat back and closed his eyes. It was all very fascinating, but suddenly he felt himself in deep water, struggling to stay afloat. He was liable to sink at any moment under the weight of accumulated knowledge, none of which seemed to be getting him anywhere nearer his goal.

'So, to sum up, it could be a break-in from outside. That would be difficult, but not impossible. Or, it could have been from inside the building, perhaps through lack of security on our part . . . '

'I'm sorry if you feel I haven't been of much help.'

'Not at all. You have been very patient. You have answered a lot of my questions. I now know a little about computers, enough to hold my own in a conversation, but . . . '

He could have added that he now knew enough to realise that the problem was even greater than he had pictured. Mademoiselle Borel was right. To all intents and purposes he was no further on than he had been when he'd arrived – as he stood up he glanced at his watch – an hour ago.

'Would you care to stay and have something to eat? I can tell you a little more about computers. Or, we can talk of other things. About what it is like being an expert on food and wine for example. The grass is always greener on the other side of the fence.'

While she was talking Mademoiselle Borel led the way back into the main room and crossed to the kitchen. As she opened the door Monsieur Pamplemousse caught sight of an orange Le Creuset pot simmering on the stove. On the working top of one of the units there was a *baguette* and alongside that a plate of *saucisson*. On another working top there was a selection of cheese.

As she lifted the lid of the pot a delicious smell wafted his way; the kind of smell that could only come from long and careful preparation and even longer cooking. It was a smell he remembered well from his childhood.

'It is only a *pot-au-feu*, but there is enough to last me for several days. You are most welcome. I cook it the way my mama did when I was small – she always served the *bouillon* on toast with the leeks.'

It had been the same in his own home. The *bouillon* from Monday's *pot-au-feu* had provided the basis for the rest of the week's meals; broth with noodles, broth with semolina and broth with rice. Then on Fridays, *potage à la fécule* – the remains of the broth thickened with cornflour. He had always hurried home from school for that.

She took a bottle of wine from a nearby rack. 'You could learn a little about Californian red at the same time. It is a Jekel Cabernet Sauvignon – Private Reserve. Or there is a Santenay if you prefer.'

Sorely tempted, Monsieur Pamplemousse hesitated. 'It is very kind of you, but I have to go. There is a great deal of work to be done. Perhaps I can take what your American friends would call a "rain check"?'

'Of course. As you see, it is a very large pot. Who knows?' As she led the way to the hall and removed his hat from the cupboard, it was her turn to hesitate. 'Would you mind if I carry on trying? Looking for a way into the computer, I mean.'

'That would be most helpful. I will keep in touch if I have any news at my end.' On an impulse he converted a hand-shake into the raising of her fingers to his lips. '*Au revoir, M'moiselle.*'

'*Au revoir.*' She waited at her door for the lift to arrive. 'Take care. I have a feeling that whoever it is you are looking for wishes to make everyone suffer for a while. If he simply wanted to hurt *Le Guide* he could have arranged for the entire program to be erased. I think he also wishes to turn the screw as well. I think it is the action of someone who is a little *en colère*.' She tapped her forehead. 'Someone with a grudge who has been brooding on it for so long it has become an obsession.'

Monsieur Pamplemousse hesitated. 'May I ask you one last question?'

'Please do.'

'The *pot-au-feu* . . . Do you seal the ends of the bones with potato to keep the marrow intact?'

'Of course.'

'Tied with string?'

'*Naturellement.*'

Monsieur Pamplemousse gave a sigh; a mixture of contentment and regret. It was echoed somewhat noisily and pointedly from inside the lift.

'That is how my mother used to make it too.'

On their way out Monsieur Pamplemousse acknowledged the glance from the hall porter with a nod. The man looked at his watch, then wrote something in a book.

Outside the block he stood for a moment, wondering what to do next. He almost wished now he had taken up the invitation to stay for a meal instead of opting for a rain check. He glanced up at the sky. From the look of it he might not have long to wait.

Somewhat inconsequentially, he suddenly remembered that it was in the Rue Raynouard that Benjamin Franklin had invented the lightning conductor.

What was the phrase Mademoiselle Borel had used? 'Assuming all external connections are correct.' She was right. In the end most problems turned out to have simple solutions. It was really a case of breaking them down into their essential elements – as with a computer.

The changes to *Le Guide* hadn't been made at random. They had been carefully thought out by someone with a good working knowledge of restaurants and what would cause the maximum amount of embarrassment. All of which would have taken time and thought.

Reaching a decision, Monsieur Pamplemousse set off in the direction of the Passy Métro station. It was time he returned to the office. If it was an 'inside job', then all his past experience told him to look for someone with a changed life style, and that brought him inexorably back to Madame Grante. He couldn't begin to suspect her of any kind of disloyalty. On the other hand, he couldn't get her out of his mind. For someone so very set in their ways, her 'external connections' had, by all accounts, gone very much awry.

There was a chance – a very slender chance – that if she did keep spare keys in her desk drawer he might find a duplicate set for her apartment. It was worth a try.

4

A Waiting Game

By the time Monsieur Pamplemousse and Pommes Frites arrived at *Le Guide*'s headquarters the gatekeeper had already gone off duty – he was probably holding court in the nearest bar, giving his version of the day's events. Using his entry card, Monsieur Pamplemousse let himself in and as they crossed the courtyard he glanced up towards the top floor. A light was on in the Director's office. There were lights coming from the second floor as well. It looked as though the occupants of the typing pool were working late. If the Director had his way they would probably be up all night.

A portable cabin containing a machine for taking passport-size photographs was standing near the main entrance. The issuing of special passes must have got under way soon after he'd left. It was closed for the night.

Unaware of the mental struggle his master had gone through earlier in the evening when he had turned down the offer of *pot-au-feu*, Pommes Frites was wearing his 'I am only a mere dog, mine is not to reason why – just lead the way and I'll follow on behind' look. It was a mixture of resignation – eyebrows slightly raised, mouth compressed, eyes focused on an imaginary horizon – and total lack of comprehension. As far as Pommes Frites was concerned, life was a simple matter of priorities. In an ideal world one should always know where one's priorities lay. The fact that for much of the time life was far from ideal was beside the point. The world was how you made it. Opportunities needed to be seized when they came your way, and although normally he would have stuck up for his master through thick and thin, sadly, on this occasion he was of the opinion that a golden opportunity had been passed up, perhaps never to return.

Ever hopeful, anticipating that amends were about to be made, Pommes Frites licked his lips as they entered the building. His euphoria was short-lived. Never one to be wreathed in smiles, he began to look even more woe begone as he followed Monsieur Pamplemousse along a route which took them not, as he had hoped, towards the canteen, the smell from which was already titillating his sensitive nostrils, but in the direction of the Accounts Department.

An air of Stygian gloom pervaded the corridors. The few people they encountered on the way spoke in whispers and barely acknowledged their presence.

When Monsieur Pamplemousse reached his destination, he opened the door to Madame Grante's outer office and peered inside. The lights were still on, but there was no sign of the new secretary. The coat rack was empty. No doubt she had another, more pressing engagement.

Closing the door behind them, he let himself into the inner office, mentally crossing his fingers and raising his eyes towards the ceiling as he did so.

It proved an unnecessary invocation to Saint Peter. Not only did his own key fit the one on Madame Grante's desk, which wasn't unduly surprising – they were all of a standard pattern and were meant to protect minor personal belongings for brief periods rather than to safeguard anything of great value – but when he opened the drawer he found the inside as neatly compartmented as the mind of its user. Pens and pencils were arranged in boxes. Paper-clips, elastic bands, a ruler, an eraser, all had their allotted place; and there, in an unmarked envelope beneath a grey lift-out plastic tray, was a set of door keys, including one which was obviously meant for the outer door to an apartment block. There was no sign of any other keys.

He was about to push the drawer shut when he noticed it felt unusually weighty. Pulling it out to its fullest extent he discovered the reason. Behind more rows of plastic containers was another copy of Cocks et Féret. It was the same edition as the one he had seen in the Director's office. He flipped through it. There were enough entries to provide a lifetime of code-words.

Monsieur Pamplemousse picked up the telephone receiver, called up an outside line, and dialled Mademoiselle Borel's number. It was either engaged or it was off the hook. Perhaps she was already hard at work trying to break into *Le Guide's* computer just along the corridor – or perhaps she was simply enjoying her *pot-au-feu* in peace and quiet.

Hearing the sound of approaching footsteps in the corridor he hastily shut the drawer, locked it, and was round the other side of the desk just as the night porter opened the outer door.

'Monsieur Pamplemousse. *Bonsoir.* Madame Grante is not working late tonight?'

'Apparently not. I can't find her anywhere.' The man looked totally unperturbed at their presence. As he turned to go, Monsieur Pamplemousse had a sudden thought. 'Were you on duty last night?'

'*Oui, Monsieur.*'

'Do you happen to know what time Madame Grante left?'

'The first or the second time, *Monsieur?*'

'You mean . . . she came back?'

'*Oui*, Monsieur Pamplemousse. I was only talking about it with my colleague just now. He saw her leave early in the afternoon – about four o'clock. He remembered it because it was so unusual – especially as she has been working late for the last few weeks. But then I was assuming she must have come back, because when her brother called for her as usual . . .'

'Her brother?' Monsieur Pamplemousse tried to conceal his surprise.

The porter gave a hollow laugh. 'That is what she liked to call him. If he is her brother, my uncle is a *rosbif.*' He used the slang term for an Englishman. 'Anyway, she must already have left when he came.'

'What time was that?'

'About nine thirty. It is in the book. I rang through but

66

there was no answer. Then he went to look for her and he came back empty-handed.'

'You let him go and look for her? By himself?'

'*Oui, Monsieur*.' The man began to look worried. 'I suppose I shouldn't have, but you know what Madame Grante is like. Besides, it wasn't as if it was the first time he'd been here.'

'Can you describe him?'

'He is about the same height as Madame Grante. A little younger, perhaps. Fairly heavily built. Well dressed – he usually wears a hat and gloves. I would say he is from the Midi. Perhaps the Rhône Valley by his accent, although he could be a Corsican. He looks a little like a . . . ' he hesitated.

'Go on?'

The man looked embarrassed. 'I would not like Madame Grante to hear me say it . . . but he looks like *un maquereau* . . . a pimp. I would not trust him with my daughter, that's for sure. Or my grandmother come to that!'

'Would you recognise him if you saw him again?'

'*Oui, Monsieur*. As I say, he has been here many times over the past few weeks. That is why I let him in.'

'And what name did he sign in the book?'

'Why, Grante of course, *Monsieur*.'

'Of course,' said Monsieur Pamplemousse drily. 'I'd forgotten. He is her brother.'

It was dark when they left the building. There was a faint drizzle in the air, so he headed up the Rue Fabert towards the taxi rank in the Place de Santiago-du-Chili.

For the first time that day he felt as though he was beginning to get somewhere. There was a glimmer of light at the end of the tunnel. It was only a very faint glimmer, and it could turn out to be an extremely long tunnel, but it was there nevertheless.

What had been said as a joke had turned out to be a distinct possibility. Perhaps Madame Grante had an '*homme*' after all. And in the circumstances, if Madame Grante had an '*homme*' then one way or another it was high time they were introduced, particularly if the porter's summing up was anything to go by.

The taxi driver took practically the same route they had walked earlier that evening, crossing the Seine by the Pont de l'Alma and then up the Avenue Marceau. Searchlights were now raking the sky above the *quai* to their right as the evening *bateaux-mouches* got ready to leave. Very soon the passengers would be dining to a running commentary on the history of Paris in four languages. The cafés in the *Place* were starting to fill.

It was strange how often life suddenly took an unexpected turn so that, within the space of a few hours, areas one hardly ever visited became a part of the daily round, rapidly becoming as familiar as the street in which one lived.

Leaving his master to his own thoughts and devices, Pommes Frites curled up beside him on the back seat and closed his eyes. He would await the call of duty, but until it came there was no sense in wasting energy needlessly.

As a precautionary measure Monsieur Pamplemousse stopped the taxi short of the Rue des Renaudes and set out to walk the rest of the way to Madame Grante's apartment. He wasn't at all sure what he expected to find when he got there, if indeed he found anything. The whole thing could turn out to be a wild-goose chase. She might well be home by now, safely ensconced in an armchair watching television. Or if she wasn't, there could be an entirely simple reason for her absence – the sudden death of a relative perhaps, an illness . . . And yet in his heart of hearts he knew none of those things rang true. Madame Grante was a creature of habit, meticulous in all matters to do with work – such behaviour would be totally out of character. And yet, and yet wasn't the whole business of her evening visitor out of character? During his years with the *Sûreté* he'd come across many occasions when, for one reason or another, people had done things totally out of character. The one thing he had learned from his experiences was never to take the behaviour of any human being for granted. His pace slowed as they covered the remaining hundred metres or so and he felt in his pocket for the keys.

Outside the block he looked first one way and then the

other. The street was deserted.

Applying the largest of the three keys to the lock, Monsieur Pamplemousse opened the outer door. The light inside the entrance hall was on. He checked the postal boxes – Madame Grante's still hadn't been emptied. There was an illuminated *minuterie* button alongside the glass-panelled inner door and as he pressed it another light came on above the lift. He tried out the Yale-type keys. The second one slid home. He held on to the first key, noting for future reference that it was the longer one of the two and by rights ought to fit the upstairs door. He took the lift this time, squeezing in alongside Pommes Frites. The only sound came from the lift motors. Even the budding saxophonist on the second floor had stopped playing.

He pressed the bell-push outside Madame Grante's apartment twice, but there was still no sound of movement. Slipping the key into the lock, he turned it gently and the door swung open to his touch, revealing a small hall. Another door on the far side stood half open and what little light there was came from a larger room beyond. He called out, but there was no response. The only sound came from the ticking of a clock somewhere nearby.

Feeling along the wall to his left, Monsieur Pamplemousse's hand made contact with a switch. As the light came on he motioned Pommes Frites to follow him in, then closed the outer door behind them and slipped the safety catch across. He had no wish to have Madame Grante return unexpectedly and mistake him for a burglar.

The living-room was much as he would have expected it to be, although after his mistake with Mademoiselle Borel he wouldn't have stuck his neck out and laid bets on it. The furniture was large and solid, old without having acquired the status of being classed as antique, although time would rectify that. It had been made in the days when oak meant what it said, not chipboard covered with the thinnest of veneers. The atmosphere felt dry and airless as though the windows had been kept shut for a long time. He registered the fact because in the office Madame Grante had a reputation for being something of a fresh-air fiend.

A large sideboard stood against one wall. The top of it was covered with framed photographs. He scanned them briefly. They were nearly all old prints, most of them in sepia. There was certainly no one remotely like the description the porter had given of Madame Grante's 'brother'. The centre-piece, in a large silver frame, showed a man in pre-war army officer's uniform. He was posing proudly beside a section of the old Maginot Line. An inscription written across the bottom half of the photograph in small, neat handwriting said: 'To Violaine, with love. Papa.' Below the words there was a single kiss. Monsieur Pamplemousse wondered if her father had survived the war. Madame Grante never spoke of her family. Alongside it was another photograph which he assumed was of her mother. It was a strong face; not someone who would have stood any nonsense. She must also have been quite a beauty in her time.

'Violaine.' He had never heard Madame Grante called by her Christian name, and he doubted if many others had either. He certainly wouldn't have dared to ask.

On the wall there were a number of old paintings of no great interest, but doubtless each had a story to tell. Amongst them was a framed certificate of competence from a school of accountancy. There was the name again – Violaine Grante.

An inlaid sewing table occupied one corner, a small *bonheur-du-jour* bureau another. Alongside it was an old Edison cabinet gramophone with a wind-up motor. Monsieur Pamplemousse opened it and looked inside. The records were all in their original sleeves; mostly artists from the early Forties. Beside them was a small tin of steel needles.

The heavy mantelpiece supported a large clock made of gilt brass inlaid with decorated porcelain panels. Flanking it were a pair of matching side urns.

In the centre of the room there was an oblong polished mahogany table protected by a crocheted runner. On it stood a bowl of freesias which had been freshly watered. Their perfume was almost overpowering.

Some french windows leading onto a balcony were shut, as

were all the other windows. He peered through the glass. The balcony ran the full width of the apartment, connecting with what must be the bedroom. At the far end on the right there was a low steel door, pock-marked with rust, which led to a fire escape. It must have been installed in the days when burglary was less of a problem, for although it was bolted on the inside, anyone with half a mind could have climbed round easily enough. Shielding his eyes from the light in the room he dimly made out the shape of a few trees in the area below; probably part of a communal garden jointly owned with those who lived in the surrounding buildings. It was starting to rain again.

In an alcove between the fireplace and the window there was a row of bookshelves. Monsieur Pamplemousse turned on a standard lamp and ran his eye along the titles. Victor Hugo, Balzac, some old school prizes, the complete works of Racine, Proust, a set of encyclopaedias; there wasn't much to choose from if you felt like a good laugh. Standing out like a sore thumb was a recent edition of a cookery book by Bocuse – put to a certain amount of use already by the look of the pages, some of which had been singled out with a strip of paper.

The top shelf was occupied by copies of *Le Guide*. The earlier ones must be collector's items, for they dated back to when Madame Grante first joined.

Idly he reached up and removed the first one. It was for 1960. *Le Guide* had gained weight since then. Fewer restaurants had been covered in those days for a start. All the same – he skimmed through the pages; it was amazing how many entries hadn't changed, particularly outside Paris. There were fewer symbols. The reports weren't quite so long. Their founder hadn't believed in wasting words.

The Director must have been an Inspector in those days. He had been brought in by Monsieur Hippolyte Duval, by then in his nineties, unmarried and childless, to be groomed for stardom as it were. Also, according to Loudier, the doyen of the Inspectors, a certain degree of nepotism had been involved. 'Family connections', he was apt to say in his dry way. But that was probably a case of provincial jealousy.

All the same, by any standards the Director had done well. Under his leadership *Le Guide* had flourished. How terrible it would be if its downfall was at hand.

But it wasn't just the future of *Le Guide* that was at stake. It was the Director too. And why the Director? Was he simply a prime target because of his position? Or was there some other reason?

On one of the lower shelves, level with an old leather armchair, Monsieur Pamplemousse came across what he had been looking for: a copy of Cocks et Féret. He opened it up. The first few pages listing the vineyards of Bordeaux had been annotated with letters corresponding to the days of the week. That was one problem solved. Mademoiselle Borel's guess had been confirmed. He was tempted to try telephoning her again with the news.

Monsieur Pamplemousse cast his eyes round the room, half expecting to see a computer terminal tucked away some-where, but apart from a radio the only concession to the world of electronics was an elderly television. It looked as if it might be a black and white model.

So far it had all been unremarkably neat and tidy. The bathroom was no exception. Everything was put away in cupboards. There were no errant tubes of toothpaste to spoil the effect; no signs of shared occupancy.

The kitchen, on the other hand, was more rewarding. It looked as though Madame Grante must have gone out in a hurry for some reason. A pile of unwashed crockery had been left in the sink to soak. The water was cold and greasy. It suggested something urgent must have cropped up. He couldn't picture her doing something like that without a very good reason. It wouldn't be in her nature. He poked around in the water. She hadn't been entertaining, that was for sure. There was only one of everything: one plate, one bowl, one set of cutlery. There was no wine glass.

Monsieur Pamplemousse glanced around the shelves. Most of the utensils were old and well worn, but there was a sprinkling of newer pieces of equipment: a Braun electric juicer and a Robot Coupé food processor, a new-looking set of Sabatier 'Jeune' professional knives in a wooden block, a mandoline for slicing vegetables, and rather surprisingly, a selection of much-used hand whisks – perhaps Madame Grante had hitherto unsuspected culinary talents?

The cupboards, on the other hand, were surprisingly bare. It looked as though someone had given them a good clear out.

He opened the refrigerator door. Somewhat unexpectedly, there was an unopened bottle of white Puligny-Montrachet in the door. It was from the *Domaine* of Henri Clerc; that from a woman who always said 'no' to a second glass of wine at the office Christmas party for fear of what it might do to her! Otherwise, apart from a few plastic pots containing unidentifiable left-overs, the shelves were once again almost bare.

Hanging on a hook fixed to the wall alongside the door were several carrier bags bearing the name of an *épicerie* in the Rue Cler near the office. Odd, given the fact that she had a thriving food market right on her doorstep. Why would she go to the Rue Cler? To save time? Because she was taking her purchases elsewhere? It was too early in the year for picnic lunches.

On his way out of the kitchen Monsieur Pamplemousse opened the lid of a rubbish chute and glanced inside. As was so often the case – his own was no exception – there were some odd scraps of paper trapped behind the flap. He was about to close it again when something about one of the pieces made him change his mind. It was part of a page torn from a large-scale map. There was a faintly familiar look about it which rang a bell in the back of his head. Someone – it didn't look like Madame Grante's writing – had marked one of the avenues with a cross. Nearby the word 'Beaumarchais' was printed. He folded the paper in half and put it in his jacket pocket for future reference.

Monsieur Pamplemousse left the bedroom until last. Somehow it felt almost like forbidden territory – and it certainly would have been '*interdit*' had Madame Grante been anywhere around; an unforgivable violation of her privacy.

The bed was large and old-fashioned with a crocheted

cover. Again, both had probably been in the family for years. On a bedside table, between a reading lamp and the telephone, there was a small doll – it looked like an Armand Marseille – and alongside that an open box of Paul Benmussa chocolates. The first layer had already gone. The sight of it made him feel hungry. He hesitated for a second or two, then resisted the temptation as he caught sight of a large thumbprint in the middle of one of the chocolates. Someone had been testing them. It looked too big to have been left by Madame Grante – and as his old mother might have said – 'you never know where it's been!'

On the dressing-table there was a bottle of Guerlain *'L'Heure Bleue'*. Again, not what Madame Grante usually wore to the office – at least, not that he had ever noticed. Once, years before, he had bought Doucette a bottle of it for Christmas. It had lasted her ages, and was only worn on special occasions.

Monsieur Pamplemousse was about to explore further when he spied something white on the carpet. Stooping down to pick it up, he reached between the legs of the dressing-table and then realised it was the note he had left on his first visit. One end was torn – torn or chewed – it was hard to say which. There was a curious series of half-round serrations – almost like tiny bites – along one edge.

He was about to hold the paper up to examine it more closely when there was a sound of flapping followed by a downward draught of air and something struck him a glancing blow on the top of the head. Almost immediately he felt a sharp needle-like pain, as if a hair had been pulled out.

Reacting in what amounted to a blind panic, Monsieur Pamplemousse automatically jumped to his feet and in so doing collided with the underneath of the dressing-table. Rolling over onto his side he clasped his head, partly in pain but also to protect it from any further blows. As he did so he made contact with something soft and wriggling. Before he had time to tighten his grasp it had gone, but not before he felt another sharp pain, this time to his index finger.

A scuffling from the direction of the doorway heralded the

arrival on the scene of Pommes Frites.

'*Comment ça va? Comment ça va?*' Hearing a strange, gruff voice calling out from somewhere near at hand, Monsieur Pamplemousse tentatively opened one eye. Pommes Frites was standing in the doorway, staring in the direction of the window as though transfixed. Had he been given to dropping his jaw in moments of stress, this, clearly, would have been one of those occasions.

Following the direction of his gaze, Monsieur Pamplemousse reacted in like manner as he found himself staring at a small blue object clinging to the top of one of the curtains.

'*Nom de nom!*' He climbed to his feet and dusted himself down.

'JoJo. JoJo. *Comment ça va?*' The gruff voice repeated itself.

Without taking his eyes off his quarry and risk losing face, Pommes Frites backed away. He shared his master's dislike of birds. They were bad enough outside, where they belonged, but at least out in the open they could be chased. Indoors, they were something else again. He fully understood Monsieur Pamplemousse's panic at having one land on his head and he had no wish to take part in a repeat performance when he would be the prime target.

Taking a leaf out of Pommes Frites' book, Monsieur Pamplemousse tiptoed towards the bedroom door and closed it behind him.

A budgerigar! That was all he needed! At least it solved the problem of the snatched note. He looked round the room and saw what he should have noticed when he first came in: a birdcage on a stand. His only excuse was that it had been partially hidden from view by the door leading to the hall. Taking a closer look he saw that it had recently been cleaned out. A new sheet of sanded paper covered the floor and that in turn had been freshly sprinkled with grit. Both the seed bowl at one end and a water bowl at the other were full. The cage door was wide open, but perhaps Madame Grante usually left it that way. Along the bottom edge of the cage there was the address of a pet shop on the Quai de la Mégisserie.

Thank goodness he hadn't opened any of the windows to let in some fresh air. If JoJo had escaped he would never have heard the last of it. He certainly wouldn't have fancied his chances of finding it on a dark, wet night in March.

Monsieur Pamplemousse sank down in the armchair beside the bookcase, wondering what to do next. If Madame Grante had left the bird flying loose she couldn't have intended being away all that long. In which case it might be better to carry on waiting for her. It would be silly to give up now.

To be on the safe side he unlocked the outer door in case she returned. It was a matter of balancing the weight of her wrath on finding herself locked out of her own apartment against having to explain why he was there and how he had managed to get in. Of the two alternatives, the latter was preferable. If she was locked out she might well call the police and he didn't want that to happen. The cat would really be out of the bag then.

As he reached across to replace the Cocks et Féret, he noticed something had fallen over in the space where it had been. Somewhat to his surprise, he saw it was a map of the Père-Lachaise cemetery. It had been folded inside out so that an inner section now formed the front cover. Part of it had been torn out. He felt inside his jacket pocket. The piece of paper fitted exactly into one of the corners.

Perhaps Madame Grante had a family grave there, and yet if that were so she would scarcely need a map to find the way – unless, of course, she'd wanted to direct someone else to the spot. From what he remembered of the cemetery it was so overcrowded you practically needed radar to find your way around.

Monsieur Pamplemousse slipped the piece of paper back into his pocket and closed his eyes.

He wondered whether he should telephone Doucette, but decided against it. For a start her sister, Agathe, always ate late and if Agathe answered the phone in no way would it be a short conversation. Anyway, Doucette was used to him being away for long periods without making contact – she wouldn't worry. All the same, he wished he hadn't thought of it. He was beginning to feel hungry.

The thought of food reminded him of Mademoiselle Borel. Was it his imagination or had she looked more than a little lonely standing in her doorway when she said goodbye? Lonely, and somehow, despite her chicness and poise, surprisingly vulnerable. He wondered if she often ate alone. If she did, it was a terrible waste. At least she didn't live on prepacked meals like a lot of women in her situation. Perhaps it was a case of 'once bitten – twice shy' and she found computers a safer bet than a husband – assuming all her external connections were correct. At least you could program them the way you wanted. He wondered if he would take her up on her offer when it was all over. What was it Brillat-Savarin had said? 'Tell me what you eat and I will tell you what you are.' It would be interesting to find out.

Monsieur Pamplemousse woke with a start as he realised a telephone was ringing somewhere. He reached out automatically and then remembered where he was.

Pommes Frites stirred in his sleep as his master blundered past towards the bedroom, rubbing his eyes as he went.

'*Allô!*' Monsieur Pamplemousse cursed under his breath as in his haste to grab the receiver he knocked over the box of chocolates.

In the background he could hear a police siren, but otherwise there was nothing.

'*Allô!*' He tried again. The only response was a click, then the line went dead.

He felt for a cord switch he had noticed earlier and as the light came on he looked at his watch. It was just after one thirty. He must have been asleep for several hours.

As he lay back on the bed for a moment gathering his thoughts, Monsieur Pamplemousse considered the matter. There had been something odd about the call, something he couldn't quite put his finger on. He wondered who could have been ringing Madame Grante at that time of night. Whoever it was must have been shocked to hear a man's voice at the other end. Probably too shocked to say anything. It sounded as though it had come from an outside box. The siren had been very close at one point.

'*Morbleu!*' He sat up with a start as he realised what had been bothering him. A siren had gone past the apartment at almost the same time – exactly in sync with the one on the telephone. Whoever it was must have been telephoning from very close by.

Turning out the light, he got up and crossed to the window. The rain was coming down even harder; it was no time to think of going out. He checked the locks on the french windows and then drew the curtains. As a further precaution he went back into the hall and set the safety catch on the front door.

Returning to the bedroom Monsieur Pamplemousse removed his jacket and tie, hung them over a chair, then lay down on the bed again and covered himself with the eiderdown. It was very unlikely that Madame Grante would return now, and if she did, then *tant pis* – too bad! He was not only tired, he was hungry. And if there was any truth in the old saying, '*qui dort dîne*' – 'He who sleeps forgets his hunger', that was precisely what he intended doing.

Half-way through plumping up the pillow, his fingers made contact with a piece of card. As he withdrew it and held it up to the light, his pulse quickened. It was a photograph of a man, and staring back at him from above the folds of a blue roll-neck sweater was a face which matched the description given to him by the night porter earlier that evening. He turned it over. On the back there was the name of a photographer. It wasn't much help – there was no address. He studied the face in greater detail, committing it to memory. The porter was right in his judgement. It was not the face of someone he would have trusted further than he could see. But what was of greater interest was an inscription across the bottom. POUR VIOLAINE – MON AMOUR. So, it hadn't been a joke after all. Madame Grante did have an *homme*. It must have turned her whole life upside-down, perhaps even made her a trifle unbalanced for a while.

He placed the photograph alongside the piece of map in his

jacket pocket, then climbed back onto the bed and closed his eyes again. Sleep came easily.

Monsieur Pamplemousse was a great believer in committing problems to his subconscious, and as he slept he wore on his face the look of someone who felt that at long last he might be getting somewhere.

5

THE GRILLING OF JOJO

Throwing politeness to the wind, Monsieur Pamplemousse elbowed his way along the already crowded Quai de la Mégisserie, weaving in and out of the trees and shrubs, packaged rose bushes, boxes of bulbs and sundry plants, until he came across the shop he was looking for. The pavement outside was already stacked with cages of varying shapes and sizes. Pigeons vied with baby goats for attention. Cocks crowed. Other creatures, like the rabbits, gerbils and guinea-pigs, carried on eating regardless. If the concerted noise coming from the occupants of the cages was anything to go by, they must have been awake for ages.

Few of the *bouquinistes* who normally plied their trade on the other side of the road seemed to have followed their example. The zinc-topped wooden bookstalls were firmly padlocked and looked as if they would remain that way for some time to come. Glancing up at the sky Monsieur Pamplemousse could hardly blame them. It looked as forbidding as the Palais de Justice on the opposite bank of the Seine, and that was saying something.

Pommes Frites followed on behind at a discreet, not to say wary distance. All was not well between dog and master. Relations were, to say the least, somewhat strained.

A student of such matters, had he been making notes, would have found his pencil racing across the page. Words such as 'nadir' rather than 'apex' would have sprung to mind when trying to describe their current mood.

Had they been interviewed, Pommes Frites would have assumed his injured expression and said quite simply that in his opinion his master had got out of bed on the wrong side.

Inasmuch as he had accidentally trodden on the chocolates, Monsieur Pamplemousse would have been the first to agree that his day hadn't exactly begun on a high note. Normally he liked to sleep with a window open and today he had woken with a headache. He was also feeling both hungry and thirsty. The refrigerator had been bare of anything which looked remotely edible at that time in the morning. He'd found the end of a *baguette*, but it was rock-hard. The coffee was instant, and therefore undrinkable, and despite the presence of the juicer, fresh oranges were conspicuous by their absence.

However, all these things had paled into insignificance when he discovered that JoJo was missing. He had spent the best part of half an hour searching high and low, calling its name and uttering tweets and other endearments, but all to no avail.

In the end there was only one conclusion to be drawn. The evidence was, he had to admit, purely circumstantial; not the kind which would have stood up in a court of law. There wasn't so much as a loose feather to be seen anywhere in the apartment, let alone on Pommes Frites' person. All the same, facts were facts.

Monsieur Pamplemousse blamed himself to some extent. He should have shut the bedroom door. Pommes Frites had been deprived of his meal and so, gently and stealthily while his master was asleep, he must have let his instincts get the better of him. There was little that could be done about it. Punishment had to be meted out at the time a crime was committed. Pommes Frites would have been both hurt and confused if his master had suddenly laid into him for no apparent reason.

The only thing to do in the circumstances was buy another bird and hope that Madame Grante might not spot the difference.

'*Attendez!*' Monsieur Pamplemousse signalled Pommes Frites to wait while he entered the shop. Pommes Frites obeyed with alacrity. He was only too well aware that his star was not exactly in the ascendancy.

Inside the shop the din was even worse. It was feeding time and the noise from puppies, dogs, kittens and a multitude of birds, all shrieking their heads off, was unbelievable. Monsieur Pamplemousse glanced around and found himself opposite a glass tank containing a python. A group of white mice snuggled contentedly in its folds for warmth, blissfully unaware of their fate. He looked the other way. Even in a pet shop the rule of the jungle prevailed.

A little further along the row, beyond some tanks of tropical fish, he saw what he was searching for: a large enclosure full of blue, grey and green budgerigars. He looked for a blue one which might pass muster for the missing JoJo. To his untutored eye, apart from variations in colour, they were all remarkably alike, but he had no doubt Madame Grante would spot the slightest difference immediately. A missing heart-shaped feather on a chin would not go unremarked.

'*S'il vous plaît?*' He summoned one of the assistants and stated his requirements.

'*Monsieur* would prefer a cock or a hen?'

It was not something he had given a thought to. 'There is a difference?'

'*Monsieur*, if you are another *perruche* there is a very great difference.'

It was hard to tell whether the man was serious or not. No doubt he'd made the same joke many thousands of times over the years. It was probably too early in the day to accompany it with a smile.

'The cocks are the best talkers.'

Anxious to escape the din, Monsieur Pamplemousse chose one at random.

The man looked down at the floor. '*Monsieur* would like it gift-wrapped?'

Monsieur Pamplemousse's heart sank. He knew he had forgotten something. Acting on the spur of the moment he had put Madame Grante's cage out with the rubbish – there was a door at the side of the lift on the ground floor of her apartment block where large objects could be deposited ready for collection. At the time he had entertained a notion of blaming it all on a burglar, but that was before he had thought of buying another bird. It had not been one of his more fortuitous thoughts; a straw of an idea, but one worth clutching nevertheless. Better than confessing to Madame Grante that Pommes Frites was probably responsible.

'Perhaps you have a cardboard box of some kind?'

'A cardboard box, *Monsieur*?' Clearly from his tone, the man was classifying his client as belonging to the last of the great spenders.

With a sigh Monsieur Pamplemousse reached for his wallet and pointed to a square cage hanging from the ceiling on the far side of the shop. It looked identical to the original.

'*S'il vous plaît.*'

The cage with its occupant, a small packet of seed, an iodised nibble and a millet spray came to over four hundred francs.

'I will throw in the sand, *Monsieur*.'

'*Merci.*' Monsieur Pamplemousse chose to ignore the contempt in the assistant's voice. '*Une fiche, s'il vous plaît.*'

Four hundred francs was four hundred francs; enough to keep Pommes Frites in food for a month. It was worth asking for a receipt. With luck he might be able to put it through before Madame Grante returned. Someone else must be holding the fort.

Ignoring the expression of disbelief which came over Pommes Frites' face when he saw his master coming out of the pet shop carrying his purchase, Monsieur Pamplemousse looked for a taxi. It was the wrong time of day and he was going in the wrong direction. He tried the rank by the Samaritaine store opposite the Pont Neuf and drew a blank. A small group of people were already waiting. The thought of going by Métro accompanied by Pommes Frites and a chattering budgerigar was not an appealing one. He wouldn't for the world have suggested that in the circumstances Pommes Frites was something of a liability – perish the thought! – but he was beginning to wish he hadn't taken his car in for a service. If he'd had an inkling of all that was going to happen he wouldn't have told the garage to take their time.

Hoping to avoid bumping into anyone he knew, Monsieur Pamplemousse crossed over the road and went down the first flight of steps leading to the river. The Seine was still brown and angry-looking. Branches of trees and other flotsam overtook him as he picked his way round puddles left by the retreating flood-waters. A tug pushing a quartet of heavily laden barges lashed tightly together overtook him. There was a car on its roof alongside a television aerial and he wondered if they would survive the next bridge. The *pénichier* at the wheel obviously thought they would, for he carried on at a remorseless seven knots, clearing the arch by inches. A small group of early-morning tourists braving the elements waved as they went past in the opposite direction. Monsieur Pamplemousse looked the other way and caught the curious gaze of a group of *clochards* sharing a bottle of methylated spirits. If staring could wear things out he wouldn't have long to go. Pommes Frites hurried on ahead, pretending he was out for a walk on his own.

What Monsieur Pamplemousse still didn't know, of course, was where Madame Grante had gone and why. She must have intended returning home within a reasonable space of time, otherwise she would have made arrangements for her bird. He couldn't believe she was so alone in the world there was no one she could have called on. A neighbour, perhaps. Or failing that, there must be places specialising in that sort of thing. No, she had left in a hurry intending to return, and so far had not done so. It was worrying.

As they crossed the little footbridge opposite the *Musée d'Orsay* he felt the first spot of rain. There was a sudden flurry of umbrellas in the long queue outside the museum. Windscreen wipers went into action on passing cars and lorries.

Looking back on it afterwards, Monsieur Pamplemousse had to admit that stopping for breakfast at a café in the Boulevard Saint-Germain in the hope that the weather would improve was a mistake, although at the time it had seemed like a good idea; a decision that Pommes Frites had heartily endorsed. He had consumed three *croissants* in the time it took the waiter to return with his master's *chocolat*. Things, in his opinion, were looking up, and not a moment too soon.

By the time the office came into view random spots had turned into a steady drizzle. The ladies of the la Varenne School of Cookery in the Rue Saint-Dominique looked up from their stoves and watched the entourage go past. It was all too clear where their sympathies lay.

As they set out to cross the vast Esplanade des Invalides, Monsieur Pamplemousse began to curse the grandiose plans of the Emperor Napoleon. They may have looked very good on paper, but he hadn't had to go out in the pouring rain – without an umbrella. Shelter was non-existent. Abandoning all attempts at keeping the cage on an even keel, he took the last fifty or so metres at a jog-trot, vying with Pommes Frites to be the first to arrive at the entrance to *Le Guide*. Pommes Frites beat him to it by a short head.

The massive double doors were shut and he was about to enter through a smaller door marked *Piétons* when he realised that someone brandishing a clip-board was hovering just inside.

'Ah, Pamplemousse!' A familiar voice boomed his name.

'*Oui, Monsieur.*' Monsieur Pamplemousse skidded to a halt in order to avoid crashing into the figure barring his way.

'I was wondering when you would honour us with your presence. You will be pleased to learn I have been holding a security check and things are going well. I trust they are with you. I shall look forward to receiving your first report.'

'*Oui, Monsieur.*' Monsieur Pamplemousse's response was terse in the extreme. It was not time for prolonging the pleasantries. He made to push his way past the Director towards the shelter of the archway only to find his way barred.

'*Pardon, Monsieur.* It is raining . . . '

'I realise that, Pamplemousse, but have you not forgotten something?'

'*Monsieur?*'

'Your pass, Pamplemousse. May I see your pass?'

'I am sorry, *Monsieur*, I have not had time to get one as yet.'

'You have no pass, Pamplemousse?' The Director made no attempt to keep the note of incredulity from his voice. 'I can hardly believe my ears. If that is the case – and I say it with equal sorrow – you may not enter. As the person responsible for security in this establishment you must realise that no exception can be made. If one began making exceptions where would it stop?'

'But, *Monsieur* . . . '

'No "buts", Pamplemousse. How do I know you are who you say you are? You stand in front of me, unshaven, bedraggled, clutching a caged *oiseau* . . . '

'How do you know I am who I say I am?' repeated Monsieur Pamplemousse, groping for the right words. He suddenly felt as if he had entered a Kafka-like dream. 'But everyone knows me.'

He turned to the man on the gate for support. 'Tell him, Rambaud.'

Rambaud responded with an all-purpose shrug, one which allowed for whatever interpretation others might like to place on it. Monsieur Pamplemousse took it to mean. '*You* know you are right. *I* know you are right. But *Monsieur le Directeur* also knows he is right and he is the boss. I have my job to think of.'

Monsieur Pamplemousse turned back to the Director. 'I was with you in your office only yesterday afternoon, *Monsieur*.'

'That is what *you* say, Pamplemousse.' The Director eyed him with a look of disfavour. 'You could be an impostor. It is not unknown.'

'How many impostors would have a dog like Pommes Frites, *Monsieur*?.

'Statistically? I would need to consult the computer.'

The Director dismissed the mathematical possibilities of such an event while he took a closer look at the bird cage. A heap of wet sand had ended up in one corner of the floor, a piece of cuttlefish lay like a stranded white whale in another.

The millet spray had long since disintegrated and an iodised nibble was about to do likewise. The bird clung forlornly by one leg to a central perch, its remaining leg tucked under an adjacent wing for comfort. It looked as though it wished it had never left the pet shop.

'That poor *oiseau* is soaking, Pamplemousse. It is a sorry sight.'

'*He* is soaking, *Monsieur*! I am soaking. Pommes Frites is soaking. That is why we wish to enter.'

'You do not have feathers, Pamplemousse.'

'Neither do I have a raincoat. I am still in mourning.' Monsieur Pamplemousse made it sound as though he wished he was mourning for the best of all reasons.

'That will do, Pamplemousse. I shall expect to see you in my office forthwith.'

'But, *Monsieur . . .* '

The Director raised his hand. 'No "buts", Aristide. A rule is a rule.'

'But if I am not allowed inside to get a pass and I am not allowed to enter without one, what am I to do? It is an *impasse.*'

'You should have thought of that in the first place, Pamplemousse. Having confirmed your new position as our chief security officer, I must admit to a sense of disappointment. I had hoped for better things.'

As the Director turned on his heels, Monsieur Pamplemousse played his first of two trump cards. 'Cocks et Féret,' he called.

The effect was both immediate and electrifying. Had he been playing the part of Lot's wife in a Hollywood extravaganza, the Director would have received rave reviews. The renewal of his contract would have been assured. He would have been typecast for ever more.

Slowly he unfroze and turned to face the gate.

'Say that again, Pamplemousse,' he exclaimed. Then he raised his hands in horror at the thought. 'No, no, please don't. Walls have ears.'

'I have not been idle, *Monsieur*. Now may I please come

in.'

'Of course. Of course.' The Director dismissed the problem summarily. 'Rambaud, escort Monsieur Pamplemousse to the photographic booth and make sure the formalities are completed with all possible speed.'

He turned back to Monsieur Pamplemousse. 'I will go on up, Aristide. Follow on as soon as you can. And please get rid of that *oiseau* on the way. I find things depressing enough as they are.'

Monsieur Pamplemousse had no wish to find himself closeted for the morning with the Director. He had other more important things to do. Sensing that he was on a winning streak, he seized the opportunity to play his second card.

'Of course, *Monsieur*. I will leave the cage out here on the pavement. No doubt the garbage men will find a home for it when they do their rounds. Although what Madame Grante will say when she hears I really don't know. It is probably her pride and joy. If she loses it she will have no one to talk to during the long winter evenings.

'You see, *Monsieur*, I spent last night at Madame Grante's apartment . . . '

'What?' The Director gazed at him as though thunderstruck. 'You spent last night with Madame Grante. I can scarcely believe my ears. I know that over the years you have acquired a "certain" reputation, which you have always chosen to repudiate, and in the past I have always given you the benefit of the doubt. But this, Pamplemousse, this is beyond the pale. No wonder you are looking the worse for wear. Shaving must have been the very last thing on your mind. As for Madame Grante, the more I hear of her behaviour, the more worried I become. Clearly she has reached a dangerous age and something has snapped. If things carry on at the present rate none of us will be able to sleep safely in our beds.'

'*Monsieur*, with respect . . . ' Monsieur Pamplemousse held up his free hand to stem the flow of words. Enough was enough.

'Respect? Respect, Pamplemousse, seems to be a singularly

ill-chosen word in the circumstances.' The Director was not to be silenced that easily.

'With respect, *Monsieur*, I did not say I spent the night *with* Madame Grante. I said I spent the night in her apartment. Madame Grante was not there. To be absolutely truthful I spent it *with* Pommes Frites. Were he endowed with the power of speech he would undoubtedly confirm the fact.'

Briefly and succinctly Monsieur Pamplemousse outlined all that had happened since he'd left *Le Guide*'s headquarters the night before, omitting only that part which involved Pommes Frites' lapse from the standards normally expected of a house guest.

To his credit, the Director listened to every word. At the end of it he stared at the cage in Monsieur Pamplemousse's hand.

'Do I understand you to say that *oiseau* belongs to Madame Grante?' he exclaimed. 'And it has the power of speech? Why on earth didn't you say so in the first place. No wonder you are carrying it around with you.'

Monsieur Pamplemousse hesitated. He could hardly tell the Director that he suspected Pommes Frites of having eaten the original inhabitant of the cage.

'Strictly speaking,' he began, wondering if hairs could be sufficiently and delicately split to avoid on the one hand retracting or modifying what he had just said and on the other hand satisfying his audience. 'When I awoke this morning and discovered Madame Grante still hadn't returned . . . '

But the Director wasn't listening. His mind was clearly racing on ahead, enjoying some new flight of fancy.

'It must be grilled.'

'Grilled, *Monsieur*?' Monsieur Pamplemousse looked suitably horrified at the thought. 'Surely a small towel would be sufficient.'

'No, no, no, Pamplemousse. I don't mean in order to dry it. I mean we must question it before it is too late. Judging from its present state its days may well be numbered. Pneumonia could set in before nightfall. We must send for a vet. There is not a moment to be lost. With luck it may reveal, albeit parrot-fashion and unwittingly, some vital scrap of information.'

'*Monsieur*, with the greatest respect, there are many things I have to do. You said yourself that time is of the essence.' Monsieur Pamplemousse wanted to say he had better things to do with his day than spend it grilling a budgerigar – especially one which hadn't as far as he knew learnt to talk.

'Leave it with me, Pamplemousse. I will personally carry out the interrogation. It will help relieve the tedium of waiting.'

The Director reached out and poked a forefinger through the bar.

'*Qui est un gentil oiseau?*'

Somewhat unjustly in the circumstances, his kindness was not rewarded in like vein.

'*Sacrebleu!*' He jumped back as if he had been shot.

'Is anything the matter, *Monsieur?*' Monsieur Pamplemousse looked suitably solicitous as the Director nursed an injured digit. 'Would you care to borrow my handkerchief?'

The Director forbore to answer. Instead, he took the cage and headed towards the steps leading to the main entrance. Monsieur Pamplemousse resisted the temptation to call out and ask if the bird ought to have a pass. It was not the right moment.

Rambaud gave another shrug, maintaining his reputation of being a man of few words. At home he probably carried out entire conversations with Madame Rambaud that way.

His photograph duly taken, a pass issued, Monsieur Pamplemousse checked in his office tray to see if there were any messages. There was one from Doucette asking him to phone, but apart from that it was empty. He tried dialling her sister's number but it was engaged.

While he was holding on he glanced out of the window. It had stopped raining. There was even a patch of lighter sky on the horizon where the sun was trying to break through. Steam was already starting to rise from his jacket which he'd draped over a nearby radiator. He reached out and felt the shoulders. It was drying remarkably well. Picking up the

contents of his pockets which were strewn over the desk, he
went through them one by one. He paused at the sight of the
map of Père-Lachaise. Perhaps it was time for another excursion? The thought triggered off another. Opening his wallet,
he removed the photograph he had found under Madame
Grante's pillow, then dialled another number.

'Administration?

'Pamplemousse here.

'Pamplemousse. *Chef de Sécurité*. May I have the home
address of the porter who was on duty yesterday evening?'

He wasn't altogether sure he liked his new title, but he
might as well make use of it while he could. One thing was
certain: as soon as the present fracas was over he would hand
over to someone else. He couldn't wait to be out on the road
again.

'*Merci.*' It was within walking distance.

Opening a desk drawer Monsieur Pamplemousse took out
a pack of disposable razors. It was high time he looked
respectable again. He glanced at his watch. It would help fill
in time before lunch.

Washed and shaved, Monsieur Pamplemousse had one
more call to make before he left the office.

The *Occupé* light was on over the darkroom door when he
reached the art department, so he left the remains of Madame
Grante's chocolates on the floor outside with a note outlining
what he needed. Given a light dusting of powder, there were
several which ought to yield quite usable thumb-prints.
Blown up, they could be of value. It was a long shot, but it
was worth a try, and it was the kind of job Trigaux revelled in
– a welcome change from his normal routine of processing
pictures of hotels and restaurants and shots of the surrounding countryside brought back by *Le Guide*'s Inspectors after
their travels.

No doubt the time was not far distant when they, too,
would be committed to an electronic memory, available at the
touch of a computer button.

A few minutes later, with Pommes Frites at his heels, he
left the building.

They had gone only a little way along the Rue Fabert when he heard the sound of someone running and his name being called out. He turned and saw the Director coming towards him. It had to be something urgent for he had left his jacket behind; an unheard-of occurrence. He wondered if something was wrong with the budgerigar.

As the other drew near he saw he was clutching a piece of paper. He looked as if he had received yet another shock.

'Thank Heaven I caught you!' The Director handed him the paper. 'Read this.'

Monsieur Pamplemousse ran his eyes over the note. It was written in block capitals in a mixture of different styles and it was brief and to the point. MADAME GRANTE IS BEING HELD PRISONER. YOU WILL NOT FIND HER. DO NOT CONTACT THE POLICE. EITHER PUBLICATION OF LE GUIDE IS SUSPENDED OR YOU WILL RECEIVE PARTS OF HER THROUGH THE POST. THE CHOICE IS YOURS. YOU HAVE UNTIL FRIDAY. THERE WILL BE NO FURTHER COMMUNICATION.

Monsieur Pamplemousse whistled. 'When did this arrive, *Monsieur*?'

'A few minutes ago. It was pushed under Rambaud's office door while his back was turned.'

'So he didn't see who did it?'

'No. I have already delivered a severe reprimand. It won't happen again in a hurry.'

Monsieur Pamplemousse fell silent. Friday! Matters were even more serious than he'd thought. It was Wednesday already.

'What does it mean, Aristide? Parts? What parts?'

'I shudder to think, *Monsieur*. An ear, perhaps. A finger. That is where such people usually start. Something easily detachable.'

'A *finger*!' The Director clutched at a lamp-post for support. 'Would anyone dare do such a thing? If it is from her right hand, think of the problems she will have when it comes to operating the computer. Keyboards can be modified, but there are limits. The whole system will suffer.'

'I think, *Monsieur*, that Madame Grante's suffering should

be our prime concern. What of her sewing and her knitting?'

The Director looked suitably shame-faced. 'You are right, Aristide. I was thinking of everyone's P39s. So much has happened over the past twenty-four hours it is hard to know where one's priorities lie. Of course Madame Grante's personal safety must come first.'

'I am also of the opinion, *Monsieur*, that when we find Madame Grante we could be well on the way to solving many of our other problems.'

'Then I must return to the *oiseau*. It may yet find itself in the witness box.'

Monsieur Pamplemousse eyed the Director dubiously. 'I doubt if a budgerigar's statement will stand up in court, *Monsieur*.'

'There is always a first time, Aristide. I have it on good authority that the testimony of a bloodhound is admissible in America. Speaking of which,' the Director glanced down. 'I take it Pommes Frites is working on the case too?'

'Of course, *Monsieur*. Rest assured we will neither of us leave a stone unturned until Madame Grante has been found.'

Monsieur Pamplemousse spoke with a confidence which he was far from feeling. In the cold light of day the Director looked drawn and haggard.

'*Comment ça va*, Chief?' He tried not to make it sound too much like JoJo.

The Director paused. 'Between you and me, Aristide, things are not so good. The girls in the typing pool are doing their best, but they are attempting the impossible. At their present rate of progress there isn't a hope in the world of publishing on time. Even with the original material it would be pushing things, but starting from scratch . . . ' He gave a dispirited shrug.

As they said goodbye and went their separate ways Monsieur Pamplemousse suppressed a shiver. For some reason he was suddenly reminded of the python in the pet store. Perhaps even now Madame Grante was snuggled up to the writer of the note, blissfully unaware of the fate he had in store for her. It was a sobering thought which only served to strengthen his resolve.

As they reached the corner of the Place de Santiago-du-Chili he paused and glanced back the way they had come. The Director appeared to be engaged in an argument with someone just inside the entrance to *Le Guide*.

Could it be that Rambaud was refusing him admission? He wouldn't put it past him. An eye for an eye, a tooth for a tooth. He would enjoy getting his own back.

Life was not without its compensations. JoJo's stand-in was enjoying an unexpected reprieve. His grilling looked as though it might be delayed indefinitely.

6

THE TOMBSTONE TRAIL

Unfurling a snow-white napkin, Monsieur Pamplemousse used it to give his moustache an anticipatory dab before tucking it in behind his shirt collar. Uttering a sigh of contentment, he settled back and took in his surroundings. Although it was barely twelve thirty, the main dining area of the restaurant was already crowded and the stools lined up in front of the bar were all taken. He was lucky to have got one of the small tables situated in the window.

He ordered a *Kir Sancerre blanc* from the waiter who had shown him to his seat and it arrived a few moments later along with a small dish of biscuits and nuts.

The pace was hotting up. Somewhere in the background he could hear the familiar sound of a kitchen hand chopping *baguettes* with a guillotine. Monsieur, presiding over the bar, was busily pouring *apéritifs* in between shaking hands with old friends and filling *pichets* and *demi-pichets* with *vin rouge*, *vin blanc* and *vin rosé* ordered from a list, unclassified and unidentified as to year, chalked on a blackboard above the counter; wines which aspired to no greater heights than that of accompanying and washing down good, wholesome food. Than which, in Monsieur Pamplemousse's opinion, there could be few better aims in life; an outlook which was endorsed without question by Pommes Frites, noisily smacking his lips as he settled himself down at his master's feet and listened to the clink of knives and forks hard at work on all sides. He, too, had a look of anticipation on his face.

Madame was busy writing down the lunch-time orders on a pad, whilst at the same time keeping a weather-eye on all that was happening around her. Other than an opening smile of welcome and a *'Bon appétit'* when the order had been brought, communication between the *patronne* and her guests was minimal. Brownie points were lost if you didn't know what you wanted by the time she arrived. Dithering caused raised eyebrows. Last-minute changes of mind gave rise to barely suppressed sighs of irritation. Time was of the essence. Her wave as she caught sight of Monsieur Pamplemousse was the equivalent of a Presidential honour.

By *Le Guide* standards there was nothing particularly special about Les Tourelles in the Rue Bosquet. The scene was probably being duplicated at that very moment in similar restaurants all over France. Waiters hurrying to and fro in their black waistcoats and white aprons, shirt sleeves rolled up in businesslike fashion to just below the elbows. The paper table-cloths laid over starched white linen. Brown panelled walls with unframed copies of turn-of-the-century posters stuck up on them. The long *banquette* covered in dark red velvet against one wall; the tables in front of it packed so close together in order to make maximum use of the available space that there was barely room for latecomers to squeeze between them; the waist-high divisions which turned the centre of the room into a group of islands surrounded by bulging coat stands.

If Monsieur Pamplemousse patronised it more than any other establishment when he was in Paris it was as much because it was handy for the office as for any other reason –, not so close that it was full of familiar faces, but not so far away that walking between the two took up an inordinate amount of his lunch time; that and the sense of timeless, unchanging permanence it always gave him. He hoped it would survive the computer age and competition from *Le Fast Food*. It would certainly need a well-programmed computer to match Madame's grasp of what was going on, and the service in most of the latter was slow by comparison.

Monsieur Pamplemousse had no problems over his order. He chose, as he almost always did, from the 78F fixed-price menu, *service compris*.

Filets de Hareng Pommes à l'Huile; 1/4 Poulet Rôti Pommes Frites; and a *Tarte aux Pommes* for himself, and the usual for Pommes Frites: a steak followed by a bone. Since a quarter-bottle of wine was included in the price of a meal it meant he would have a whole half-bottle to himself. He chose the red. Pommes Frites would be more than happy with a splash in his bowl of water; what was known as an *abondance*.

'*Saignant?*' Madame wrote down the second part of his order without batting an eyelid, then automatically slipped the bottom copy of the bill under an ashtray for the waiter to see when he brought the basket of bread.

'*Oui, s'il vous plaît.*' Pommes Frites wouldn't mind if his steak was underdone or not, though if pressed for a decision he would probably have opted for whichever method took the least time. Gastronomically, his master's present case had been a disaster area so far. Not at all up to par.

While waiting for his *hareng* to arrive Monsieur Pamplemousse mused on his visit to the night porter. The man's reaction to the photograph had been revealing, for he had added one useful piece of information. It was to do with the man's attire. Madame Grante's brother didn't always look quite as immaculate as he had described earlier. On the night in question he had looked much as he did in the picture. He'd been wearing a dark blue roll-neck sweater, to which could be added light blue jeans, a black leather jacket, and rope-soled shoes.

He also had a nervous tic in his right eye.

'Why didn't you tell me?'

The man had looked injured. 'You didn't ask me, *Monsieur*. You only asked me what he usually looked like.'

To which there had been no answer.

'Assuming all external connections are correct.' Martine Borel's phrase came back to Monsieur Pamplemousse as he took the photograph out of his pocket and had another look. One connection was certainly missing: where the picture had been taken; it would be nice to know. It was obviously a studio shot and the only clue was the name of the photographer on the back. It would be like looking for a needle in a haystack, unless . . .

In between the *hareng* and the *poulet* Monsieur Pamplemousse left his table for a moment to make a telephone call.

'Mademoiselle Borel? *Comment ça va?* I hope I am not interrupting you.

'Me? It is hard to say. I have a few leads but not much time.'

'You could do something for me on your *Minitel*.

'I need to know the location of a photographer. I have the name, but no other details. Is that possible?

'No. I will give you my office Fax number. If you have any luck you can let me know there.

'*Merci.*' Once upon a time he would have used the *pneumatique* system. Using compressed air to propel messages to their destination via a network of underground pipes had seemed the ultimate in speed and efficiency. Now, he didn't even know if it was still in use. Perhaps it was yet another casualty of the computer age.

The *poulet* arrived just as he got back to his table. It was large and crisp and succulent; doubtless Pommes Frites would be only too pleased to help him out if he had problems. The mound of accompanying *frites* were equally crisp, verging on the golden; the bread basket had been topped up.

Between mouthfuls he gazed out of the window at the people hurrying past. Occasionally they stopped to study the menu or to peer inside before going on their way.

His thoughts turned again to Madame Grante. Since the message had been delivered by hand, the chances were that the man had done it himself – by now Monsieur Pamplemousse was convinced they were dealing with one person, although if he'd been asked to give his reasons he would have been hard put to say why; it was simply a hunch. If he was right, whoever it was would hardly have entrusted the job to anyone else – he would have wanted to make sure that it got there safely. He might even have got a kick out of doing it himself; there was a kind of sadistic element to all that had happened so far. In which case the person responsible was probably at large somewhere in Paris. But where in Paris? For all Monsieur Pamplemousse knew he could be sitting in the same restaurant at that very moment watching him from another table.

It was all very well the Director saying don't bring the police in, but there could come a point when they would have to. The whole thing had escalated beyond the mere good of *Le Guide*. Madame Grante's life was now at stake. If they left it too long they would be abused for not having done it sooner. The police were no better than anyone else at working miracles.

After the *tartes aux pommes* Monsieur Pamplemousse ordered a *café* and at the same time called for his bill. They arrived together.

Back at the office everyone else in his section was still out for lunch. He was glad in a way. He wasn't in the mood for small talk.

A large manila envelope awaited him on his desk. It was plastered with DO NOT BEND labels. Trigaux must have worked through his lunch break.

Monsieur Pamplemousse picked up the phone and called his contact at the *Sûreté*.

'Jacques? Aristide here.

'*Oui, bien, merci.*

'You might have told me it was *Mademoiselle*. I was expecting a *Monsieur* Borel.'

He got the same reply he'd been given by the night porter. 'You didn't ask me.' It was another case of 'assuming all external connections are correct.' He was stuck with the phrase now for ever more.

'*Oui.* She was very charming and helpful.' While he was talking, Monsieur Pamplemousse cupped the receiver under his chin and undid the flap of the envelope.

'Jacques, there is another small favour I would like to ask. It is a long shot, but I have some blow-ups of a thumb-print.

'Of course. When it is all over.

'At the restaurant of your choice.'

Holding the photograph between thumb and forefinger, he

shook the envelope free. As he did so a piece of paper fell out and fluttered to the table. It was a note from Trigaux.

'Next time you have any chocolates you need photographed, try leaving them further away from the door.'

Monsieur Pamplemousse stared at the picture. It was in colour. Oozy, sickly, and almost uniformly chocolate brown. It was like looking at a child's idea of a moonscape. The flat area in the centre showed clearly where Trigaux had stood.

'*Qu'est-ce que c'est?*' He suddenly realised there was a disembodied voice in his right ear.

'*Non*. Forget it.

'*Oui*. I will be in touch.'

Monsieur Pamplemousse put the receiver down and buried his head in his hands. He stayed where he was for a while, only vaguely aware of the fact that a girl had entered the room through a door at the far end and was coming towards him. She was clutching a piece of paper and she looked in a hurry.

'Monsieur Pamplemousse. I am glad I caught you. We thought you might not be coming back.'

He took the piece of paper and glanced at it mechanically. The word URGENT was stamped in red across the top.

The typed message was short and to the point. Three towns were listed: Rennes, Nice and Belfort. Each was followed by an address. '*Bonne chance* – Martine' had been added in ink.

The miracles of modern science! Where would it all end? At one time such a task would have taken many people weeks of painstaking work sifting through directories.

He glanced up and realised to his surprise that the girl was still there.

'There is no reply. Unless . . . ' Monsieur Pamplemousse paused for a moment. 'Send a message back saying, "*Merci*." You could add the word "Bordeaux" if you like.'

If Martine was still working on the code-word to enter the computer, she deserved a clue. It was too late for the information to do any harm even if it got into the wrong hands. Doubtless a new code would have to be devised anyway.

'I will do that straight away, Monsieur Pamplemousse.'

The girl still showed no sign of leaving. She looked embarrassed.

'Well? What is it?' He tried not to sound too impatient.

'It is about Madame Grante, Monsieur Pamplemousse.'

'Madame Grante?'

'We were discussing your message . . . '

'We? Who are "we"?'

'The other girls in the Communications Room and myself.'

'How do you know it concerns Madame Grante?'

'We put two and two together and since you are working
on the case and it was marked "urgent" . . . '

Monsieur Pamplemousse gave a sigh. So much for security
and confidentiality. The Director would not be pleased if he
knew!

'And what conclusion did you reach?'

'It isn't exactly a conclusion, Monsieur Pamplemousse. It is
just that it is a funny coincidence.'

Monsieur Pamplemousse tried to conceal his growing
impatience. 'A coincidence? Tell me, what coincidence?'

'Well, you see, last summer Madame Grante went on
holiday to the Jura, and when she came back she was all
different . . . '

'Different? How do you mean – different?'

'Well, it is hard to say. She was somehow . . . nicer, and
she seemed more approachable. I remember she brought us
back a bottle of Suze and some *tarte au fromage*. I had never
tasted Suze before.'

Suze. He hadn't had any himself for a long time. It was an
acquired taste, popular with commercial travellers and others
who had to stand lots of drinks, according to George
Simenon's Maigret. The *gentiane* from which it was made had
medicinal qualities and it was low on alcohol.

'Anyway, we decided she must have met someone while
she was there.'

Monsieur Pamplemousse sat up. He was suddenly all ears.

'And?'

'Well, it didn't last for very long. After a while she gradually dropped back into her old ways again. Worse, if anything

– and we all thought that was that. Then, just recently, it happened again, only this time we really knew there was something going on. She started having flowers on her desk and once . . . ' The girl began to blush again.

'Go on.'

'Well, once someone saw her coming out of that shop in the Rue Cler, you know . . . '

Monsieur Pamplemousse didn't know, but he didn't want to lose face either. He suspected it might be the one with the frilly-packed window. It had one of those fashionable 'In' names which could have applied to almost anything. He wondered what it was all leading up to.

'So, as I was saying, when we saw the message and the list of places we put two and two together. Belfort is in the Jura, which is where Madame Grante went to on her holiday, and well, we thought you might like to know.'

'You did well. *Merci.*'

The girl paused at the door. 'Madame Grante *is* going to be all right, Monsieur Pamplemousse? I mean, she's a funny old thing at times, but she's got a heart of gold really. Especially if anyone's in trouble. I think she's probably very lonely, so she puts up all sorts of barriers and pretends she doesn't mind.'

As the girl made her exit, Monsieur Pamplemousse gazed out of the window, lost in thought. Communication! Despite all man's endeavours, despite the invention of the computer or perhaps even because of such things, communication on its simplest level remained the great problem in the world. There he had been, living in his own little world, wrestling with his problem, and in another part of the very same building a group of young girls had been sitting around thinking about it as well, putting two and two together and coming up with one of the answers he needed. If it hadn't been for the Fax message they might never have told him.

Belfort! Opening one of the drawers he took out a copy of *Le Guide* and leafed through it. Belfort was just a name, somewhere he had yet to visit. He found it on page 221. It boasted one major hotel – the Hôtel du Lion, several lesser ones with varying degrees of comfort, two restaurants with a Stock Pot, and a sprinkling of smaller ones. He wondered if Madame Grante had stayed at any of the ones listed, and if so, which. He made a note of the names on his pad, then put the book away.

'Ah, Pamplemousse.' Outside in the corridor the first person he bumped into was the Director. He had his right arm in a sling and he looked in a bad mood. There was a second finger in plaster.

'Pamplemousse, that *oiseau* is as ill-tempered as its mistress. They say pets grow to be like their owners. I fear it may never yield up its secrets. It hasn't uttered a single word since I last saw you. Its lips are sealed.'

'Its lips, *Monsieur*, but clearly not its beak.' Monsieur Pamplemousse glanced down at Pommes Frites. He must study his own face more carefully next time he was in front of a mirror to see if there were any changes. There could be worse fates.

The Director looked at him suspiciously. 'I have just been to see Sister. She has inoculated me against psittacosis. One never knows where its beak may have been.'

'A wise precaution, *Monsieur*. I understand the disease is highly contagious. One cannot be too careful.'

'Perhaps you would care to have a go, Aristide. You are more skilled in the art of third degree than I.'

Monsieur Pamplemousse hastily declined the offer.

'Pommes Frites and I are off to the Père-Lachaise cemetery, *Monsieur*.'

The Director turned momentarily pale. 'Not bad news, I trust? Nothing to do with . . . '

'It is hard to say, *Monsieur*. I will let you know if anything develops.'

As they left the office Monsieur Pamplemousse decided to take a chance and catch the *autobus* to Père-Lachaise. The 69 normally had an open platform at the rear and because it started near by in the Champ-de-Mars it was rarely full.

His ploy worked. It wasn't the first time. Appreciating what his master required of him, Pommes Frites waited in a convenient doorway near a stop in the Rue Saint-Dominique until the *autobus* drew up alongside. There were no more than half a dozen passengers, all of them facing the front. As Monsieur Pamplemousse climbed aboard and flashed his pass, momentarily distracting the driver away from his rear-view mirrors, Pommes Frites slipped quickly over the rail at the back and lay down out of sight. With the weather as it was, the *autobus* would need to get very crowded before anyone else was hardy enough to join him. But just in case, Monsieur Pamplemousse stationed himself on one of the rear seats with his legs stuck out across the door and his hand at the ready so that he could give the appropriate signal to abandon ship if need be.

He wanted time to think and somehow he always found the autobus more profitable in that respect than the Métro. It was somehow more soothing; there were fewer distractions. On the Métro people tended to watch you thinking for want of something better to do.

There was an element about the sabotaging of *Le Guide* which was bothering him. It had been nibbling away at the back of his mind all day.

So far he had been assuming – and he had no doubt that others, including the Director, had made the same assumption – that the version which was now committed to the computer's memory was a revised version of the forthcoming publication. He'd assumed it for the very simple reason that there had been so many other things on his mind he hadn't even bothered to sit down and think it through.

But if that wasn't the case – if it was based on last year's guide, for example – did that make any difference? It would mean it could have been prepared over a long period, rather than in the brief time between finalisation and the launch party. It would then have been a comparatively simple task either to substitute a bogus *disque* the night before – presumably only a matter of moments – or to transfer it electronically. He had no idea how long that would take.

In the Rue de la Roquette they had an encounter with a parked lorry. The road was narrow at that point and they were unable to pass. A short argument ensued which ended as it had begun with the driver of the *camion* refusing to move until he had finished unloading.

The driver of the *autobus* picked up his telephone and spoke briefly. A minute or so later there was the familiar sound of a police siren.

The lorry driver climbed into his cab and drove off. Doubtless he, too, felt himself a victim of the computer age.

They arrived at the main entrance to Père-Lachaise without further incident. Glancing up at the gathering rain-clouds, Monsieur Pamplemousse decided to remain where he was while the *autobus* skirted round the outside wall of the cemetery, climbing the steep hill towards the entrance on the far side. It would save making a similar climb on foot once he was inside the gates. Taking advantage of the general exodus towards the middle as they approached the terminus in the Place Gambetta, Pommes Frites made his own disembarkation arrangements and was already waiting on the pavement by the time the doors opened. From the way he behaved as he caught sight of his master he could have been sitting there for hours.

As they approached the entrance to the cemetery Monsieur Pamplemousse saw a woman attendant in a blue uniform peering out from her hut. She eyed Pommes Frites suspiciously as they drew near. Monsieur Pamplemousse sighed. It was yet another hazard to be overcome. For a country which allowed dogs into restaurants up and down the land and which supported a thriving industry catering to their many needs and demands, there were a remarkable number of no-go areas. He pretended not to have noticed the CHIENS INTERDITS sign.

Treading the fine line between what some might take as a compliment and others might misconstrue, Monsieur Pamplemousse raised his hat.

'*M'moiselle.*' He'd guessed right. The woman softened immediately.

Looking round as though to make sure no one could overhear, he leaned forward conspiratorially. As he did so he encountered a strange smell; a mixture of stale body odour and damp uniform in the ratio of two to one. It was not a pleasant experience. Reaching inside his jacket pocket with one hand, he motioned towards Pommes Frites with the other.

'*Permettez-moi, M'moiselle*? He was a great fan of the late Edith Piaf.'

'I see no *chien, Monsieur.*'

Monsieur Pamplemousse withdrew a note from his wallet. 'In that case may I invest in a map.'

The woman's hands closed around the note, held his own for rather longer than was strictly necessary – long enough for Monsieur Pamplemousse to realise that in his haste he had mistaken a hundred franc note for a twenty – then slipped it inside the top of her jacket. Without taking her eyes off him, she reached towards a shelf just behind the door of her hut. As she did so he noticed another sign: POURBOIRES INTERDIT.

Thanking her for the map, Monsieur Pamplemousse considered the situation. Patently, the transaction was considered to be at an end; negotiations as to price were not about to be entered into. For the briefest of moments he wondered whether to make up for the lack of change in some other way. He decided against it. It wouldn't do to press his luck too far. She didn't look the type of woman who gave receipts, and picture postcards were conspicuous by their absence.

'*Vous êtes très gentille, M'moiselle.*' The compliment went the way of the note.

'*Monsieur* will find the grave of Edith Piaf near the *Monuments aux Résistants et Déportés* at the far end.'

Monsieur Pamplemousse felt the woman's eyes boring into the back of his neck as he set off at right angles to the way he had intended going. Pommes Frites was already bounding along on a parallel course to his own, picking his way sure-footedly in and out of the gravestones, pausing every so often to make sure his master was still in sight, or to leave his mark.

Monsieur Pamplemousse wondered idly if his friend might encounter the giant cat said to haunt the place, albeit in search of young maidens. It was the kind of day for it: dark and gloomy. If they did meet up there would be hell to pay. Hair and fur would fly.

As soon as he could, he turned right and set off up the hill, past the memorial to Oscar Wilde, to where Pommes Frites stood waiting for him. Avoiding the vast bulk of the *Columbarium*, he took a short cut. Simone Signoret lay undisturbed but not forgotten to his right. Further still there was the usual small group gathered in silent worship around the memorial to the faith-healer Kardec. Eyes tightly closed, a middle-aged woman clung to the stone as though she was part of it. She looked as though she had been there for hours. He could have done with a bit of such blind faith himself.

Having reached the highest point, he made his way down to the little chapel and paused in the gardens for a moment in order to compare his own torn-out piece of map with the one he had just bought. As he had thought, the marked area came from the older part of the cemetery, hardly changed since the beginning of the nineteenth century, when the architect Brongniard had landscaped it, leaving the lime and chestnut trees from the original Jesuit gardens, but constructing a network of cobbled lanes and winding gravelled paths leading out from where he was standing. Abélard and Héloïse were buried somewhere near the bottom of the hill, along with Chopin, Cherubini and countless others whose gravestones marked the passage of history, and where Balzac used to wander 'to cheer himself up'.

Monsieur Pamplemousse looked around as he rotated the map in order to get his bearings. Not many people were braving the weather that afternoon. The few hardy ones were mostly hidden beneath umbrellas, for it had started to rain again. He wished now he had brought one himself. If he'd thought, he could have borrowed one from the office.

There was a continuous roar from the wind in the trees and he found it hard to hold the map out straight. A sprinkling of dedicated tourists peered at their guidebooks in the dim light as they picked their way resolutely along sodden gravelled side-paths trying to reach their objectives before the gates closed. He caught an occasional glimpse of some lone person

– almost always a woman – paying her respects to a loved one. You would need to miss someone very badly to be there on such a day. It wouldn't be long before the usual quota of exhibitionists, fetishists, grave-robbers, necrophiliacs, perverts, voyeurs and other bizarre inhabitants of the potter's fields put in an appearance.

He set off in a south-westerly direction along the Avenue de la Chapelle, then turned left, following a path which took him past the tombs of La Fontaine and Molière. As far as the eye could see there were thousands and thousands of tiny stone properties, many of which looked as though they had long since been abandoned, their iron gates either rusted away or hanging drunkenly by a single hinge. In parts it was more like a repository for ancient telephone kiosks and *pissoirs* rather than a cemetery. A sodden-looking black cat appeared from behind a gravestone, then beat a hasty retreat when it saw Pommes Frites.

Monsieur Pamplemousse found what he was looking for in an area occupied by some of the more illustrious Marshals of France. It somehow fitted in with the Director's preferred image. He saw the names of Ney and Masséna and Lefebvre.

The discovery wasn't a total surprise; in a way he had half expected it. All the same, it still gave him a strange feeling to see the name Leclerc engraved in the stone above the Director's family motto: *Ab ovo usque ad mala*. He supposed it meant from the egg to the apples – from beginning to end, after the Roman habit of starting a meal with eggs and ending it with apples. Given the Director's present occupation it was an apposite choice. Interestingly, the name was spelt in its simplest form, without the letter 'q' at the end. It bore out Loudier's theory that the Director himself had added it at some point in time.

The vault was better kept than most of those around it. On one side the inscription CONCESSION A PERPETUITE was followed by a number and a date – 1780 – but it had clearly been well maintained; the stonework was clean and the ironwork was freshly painted. Monsieur Pamplemousse climbed up a small flight of steps and peered through a glass-backed ornamental door grill. There was a vase of fresh flowers standing on a plinth at the back, and the floor looked as though it had been recently swept. Otherwise the inside was bare. Around the walls there were names engraved. The Director's grand-father had died not so long ago at the age of ninety-one – he remembered hearing about it at the time. Two uncles had died in the war. The Director's father must be still alive, the date of birth – 1892 – had been entered, but the space which had been left to record the date of his death was blank.

While his master was at the top of the steps, Pommes Frites busied himself at the bottom. There were a number of inter-esting, not to say unusual scents to be found on the ground around the tomb. Many of them were quite recent. Not for nothing had he won the Pierre Armand trophy as the best sniffer dog of the year during his time with the Paris *Sûreté*. Had Pommes Frites, like his human counterparts on other courses of a not dissimilar nature, kept a notebook, then he would have made entries under a variety of headings. Earth scents, which covered crushed worms and other insects, not to mention cracked and bruised vegetation. Individual scents, with subdivisions relating to Human Scent, Sex (m. or f.); and Regional Scents, covering each and every part of the body. The third category, Additional Scents, embraced types of footwear and their composition – whether they were made from leather or rubber – shoe cream, occupational scents and the kind of clothing worn.

Making full use of the long ears and hanging lips with which nature had endowed him, Pommes Frites concentrated first of all on trapping body scents, feeding them into a system which was a million times more powerful than that of any human. He registered the fact that someone whose odour he didn't immediately recognise had been very busy. Earth scents didn't yield a great deal, largely on account of the nature of the terrain. Additional Scents was the most reward-ing; there were several he couldn't immediately identify – but all, animal, vegetable and mineral, were duly separated and filed away in his memory for later use should the need arise.

The task completed, his mental 'in-tray' empty once again,

Pommes Frites marked the spot in time-honoured fashion and stood waiting patiently on the path, wondering what would happen next and why his master was looking so puzzled.

The simple fact was that Monsieur Pamplemousse looked puzzled because nothing he had seen so far offered up any clue as to why the piece had been torn out of the map. Perhaps it was simply, as he'd first thought, a reminder as to the exact position of the Director's family tomb. But if that was the case what was it doing in Madame Grante's apartment? It wasn't until he turned to make his way down the steps again that he saw what could be the answer: just to the right of the doorway the Director's name had been chiselled into the stone. It was followed by the beginnings of a date – the day and the month, but not the year. Perhaps whoever was responsible had been caught in the act. It was the same date as had appeared in the *journal* several days previously announcing the Director's death.

Monsieur Pamplemousse took a closer look. The work had obviously been carried out by a portable cutter of some kind; the marks were those of a saw rather than a chisel. It wasn't nearly so professional-looking as it had seemed at first sight. Nicks where the blade had overrun were crudely etched in – probably by a felt-tipped pen.

He stood up and considered the matter. If it was a joke, then it was in very poor taste. And if it wasn't a joke? In his heart of hearts he knew that whoever was responsible wasn't joking. It fitted in with all that had gone on before. The piranha fish, the announcement in the paper, the sabotaging of *Le Guide*, the kidnapping of Madame Grante; no one would go to that much trouble unless they were in deadly earnest. And if they were that serious then there was no time to be lost.

Faced with the distinct possibility that if he didn't act quickly he might have more than one corpse on his hands before the week was out, Monsieur Pamplemousse reached for his notepad and pen. It was clutching at straws, but he had to grab hold of something. Anything was better than nothing.

The chances were that anyone so totally obsessed with detail would want to come back and finish the job. It needed something to arouse his opponent's interest without giving anything away. He made two attempts, screwing both up in disgust before he finally struck the right note: MEET ME ON THE TERRACE OF AUX DEUX MAGOTS. 10.00 TOMORROW. CARRY A COPY OF LE GUIDE.

If he read his adversary correctly he wasn't someone who would risk leaving such an invitation unanswered. The alternative was to hang around in the rain in the hope that someone might eventually turn up. It wasn't an attractive prospect.

The suggestion that whoever read the message should carry a copy of *Le Guide* was a master-stroke. It added a certain bizarre, yet at the same time logical note to the proceedings – in keeping with the way the other's mind must be working.

Mindful of *Le Guide*'s circulation figures and the possibility of confronting some innocent tourist, he added a post-script. OPEN AT PAGE 221!. He plucked the figure out of the air, much as he might have picked a raffle ticket. It wasn't until some time later that he realised why he had chosen it.

Carefully making sure the first few words of his message were visible, Monsieur Pamplemousse slipped the note into the plastic cover of his season ticket in order to protect it from the rain and placed it under a stone at the bottom of the door. It would be out of sight to any casual passers-by, but clearly visible to anyone interested enough to take a closer look.

Lost in thought, Monsieur Pamplemousse set off towards the Avenue Circulaire along a route which would take them back to where they had started. Pommes Frites followed on behind wearing his enigmatic 'mine is not to reason why' look. Left to his own devices he would have gone in quite the opposite direction, but he was too well trained to protest. His moment would come. Every dog had its day. No doubt his views would be sought when the time was ripe. He only hoped it wouldn't be too late.

Anyway, there were soon other problems to contend with. As they reached the *Mur des Fédérés* in the south-east corner of the cemetery, scene of the Paris Commune's final bloody stand when the last 147 insurgents were cornered and shot, it started to rain in earnest. There weren't even any empty tombs to provide shelter; it was a part where flat grave stones predominated. He tried sheltering beneath a couple of spindly coniferous trees, but they were worse than useless. It was like standing under a colander. Any admirers of the late Edith Piaf had long since disappeared.

Making a break for it, he dashed towards the gates. The woman attendant beckoned to him invitingly from the shelter of her hut as they ran past. In her plastic bonnet she looked like an elderly pixie who had seen better days. Monsieur Pamplemousse pretended he hadn't seen her, which wasn't difficult, for by now the rain was coming down in sheets. Their departure coincided with a loud clap of thunder almost overhead.

Thinking about it afterwards, Monsieur Pamplemousse was inclined to draw a veil over the rest of the day; some things in life were best forgotten. Soaked to the skin; his already heavy suit feeling like a ton weight; failing miserably in an attempt to board an already over-crowded *autobus* whose passengers took one look at Pommes Frites and then raised their voices in a unanimous vote of protest – totally unappreciative of the fact that in similar circumstances, they too would have wished to shake themselves dry; unable to find a taxi – doubtless they had all gone home to escape the worst of the weather; their way barred on the Métro by a group of roving Inspectors anxious to justify their salaries whilst themselves sheltering from the storm; it felt like a bad dream during which one avenue after another was barred to them. He was past caring. There had come a point where nothing mattered any more.

If he had thought about it at all he would have gone back to his own apartment and got a change of clothing; but he didn't, so there was no point in wishing he had. Like a homing pigeon, he headed for Madame Grante's instead. He was far too wet to notice that in his absence someone had collected the mail from the box in the hall.

Never had anywhere looked more welcoming. As soon as they were safely inside her apartment, Monsieur Pamplemousse emptied the pockets of his suit and spread them out over the living-room table. The recent soaking had started where the first one had left off. It was doubtful if his suit would ever be the same again. He found the remains of a disintegrated mothball where his wallet had been and immediately wished he hadn't. It would probably take days for the smell to go away. Removing his jacket, shirt and trousers, he draped them over a clothes-hanger, then looked around for somewhere to hook it. The hall was out of the question. He tried hitching it over a drawer knob in the kitchen, but in no time at all there was a pool of water over the floor which grew larger with every passing moment. In the end he settled on the balcony. The wind was blowing from the west and that side of the building was sheltered from the rain.

He shivered as he went back inside, locking the door behind him and drawing the curtains. It was no night to be out half-dressed. He made his way into the living-room, switched on the electric fire, and was about to undress further when he realised Pommes Frites was behaving strangely. He was pacing up and down, sniffing here, there and everywhere, looking first in the hall, then in the bedroom and the kitchen; nothing escaped his scrutiny.

Monsieur Pamplemousse glanced around. He prided himself on having a photographic memory, and as far as he could see everything was exactly where he had left it that morning. Yet there was no denying the look of intense concentration on Pommes Frites' face. Clearly something was amiss. Equally certain was the fact that whatever or whoever was responsible was no longer in evidence.

So in the spirit of better safe than sorry, Monsieur Pamplemousse went the rounds, lowering the shutters on all the windows and putting the catch on the front door to be on the safe side. Then he carried on as before.

Removing the rest of his clothing, he filled the kitchen sink with water and left it to soak. Then he went into the bathroom and turned on the taps.

Following on behind, Pommes Frites sat watching in thoughtful mood while his master lay back, luxuriating in the warmth of the water as it crept higher and higher. He knew what he knew, and in his humble opinion having a bath was not the most important thing in the world at that moment in time, but there was no accounting for the way human beings behaved. They often did the strangest things.

It wasn't long before the inevitable happened. Monsieur Pamplemousse began to sing. It was another thing that was a constant source of amazement to Pommes Frites: the odd noises human beings made when confronted with a bath full of water.

Suddenly they both froze as a voice came from the other room. Monsieur Pamplemousse scrambled to his feet. He reached out for a towel only to discover there wasn't one. In desperation he grabbed hold of the first thing he could find. As he climbed out of the bath he caught sight of his reflection in a mirror.

There was only one consolation. Whoever the voice belonged to, it was patently not Madame Grante. She wouldn't take kindly to the sight of her best flannel being used for the purpose to which he had just put it.

7

Rendezvous At Aux Deux Magots

Signalling Pommes Frites to remain where he was, Monsieur Pamplemousse crept towards the bathroom door and peered through the crack. Hairs bristling, muscles quivering, ready to spring into action at the blink of an eyelid, Pommes Frites obeyed instructions, albeit with a certain amount of reluctance. From where he was crouching his master looked more than usually vulnerable and in need of care and protection. Bringing up his rear was not, in Pommes Frites' opinion, the best way to go about things.

'*Allô. Qui est là?*'

'*Allô. Qui est là?*' Monsieur Pamplemousse gave a start and then relaxed. The voice echoing his words from the other room had a familiar, if not particularly welcome ring to it.

He flung open the door and was greeted by a fluttering of wings as something small and blue detached itself from a nearby picture rail and took off in a wild excursion round and round the room, careering into things as it went, before finally settling on a curtain at the far end.

It was all he needed to make his cup of unhappiness complete – a *oiseau*! And not just any old *oiseau*, but clearly, from the few words it had uttered to date, the genuine article. Where JoJo had been hiding and what he had been doing during the interim period was neither here nor there; a mystery which would probably never be solved. But there he was, as large as life and twice as noisy, gazing at him through beady, panic-stricken eyes. It was a problem Monsieur Pamplemousse was in no mood to deal with at that moment, even if he'd been able to. For a split second he was sorely tempted to take the easy way out and open the windows; what the eye didn't see the heart didn't grieve for, but his better nature caused him to have second thoughts. It was hard to envisage, but Madame Grante probably loved JoJo.

There was a stirring from inside the bathroom as Pommes Frites, tiring of his restricted view of the world and unable to contain his curiosity a moment longer, joined his master in the doorway. Monsieur Pamplemousse immediately felt a pang of remorse. That he could have thought the worst about his friend was unforgivable. He reached down and gave him a conciliatory pat.

Pommes Frites, for his part, looked as though he would have been only too pleased to make up for things and in so doing justify his master's earlier mistake. His better nature did not extend to love of birds, domesticated or otherwise. He licked his lips. Birds were for chasing.

Bereft of his clothes, clad only in an ill-fitting silk dressing-gown belonging to Madame Grante which he had found hanging behind the bedroom door, his inner man scarcely replenished by a single slice of toasted stale *baguette* which he shared with Pommes Frites, Monsieur Pamplemousse spent an unhappy evening. The high spot came when, having washed his underclothes, he hung them out on the balcony alongside his suit. With luck they would be dry by morning. After that, time hung heavily on his hands. At around nine o'clock he had a second slice of toast. Pommes Frites devoured his half in a single crunch, then sat watching through soulful unblinking eyes while Monsieur Pamplemousse eked out his portion until, unable to stand it a moment longer, he sacrificed the last corner.

He toyed with the idea of ringing Doucette to see if she could organise something, but it was late and explanations as to why he was sitting in Madame Grante's apartment *sans* his clothes would be tedious in the extreme and might not be believed.

He tried watching television for a while, but it was a panel game, '*Chiffres et Nombres*', and he wasn't in the mood. Tino Rossi singing '*Mon Pays*' began to pall after the fourth playing, and as the evening wore on he found difficulty in sharing Edith Piaf's philosophy of having no regrets.

Why on earth he hadn't gone home first he didn't know. Well, he did know, of course. Once he had his nose into a case nothing else mattered. But at least if he'd gone back to his own apartment he could have changed into some other clothes and used the time to better advantage. But doing what? He had done everything he could think of for the moment. It was now a matter of waiting. Waiting to see what his opponent's next move would be. Despite the first message saying there would be no further communication, he couldn't believe that was true. He'd already broken that vow once. He must be just as much on edge as everyone else, probably even more so. In his experience it was always the same; it was a battle of nerves – each side waiting to see if the other broke first. But would the next communication be in the form he'd threatened – a part of Madame Grante? The chances were that even if he meant what he'd said at the time, when it came to the crunch it would only be used as a last resort; certainly not until the date of *Le Guide*'s publication had come and gone.

If only Trigaux hadn't stepped on the chocolates. The way he was feeling he would even have eaten the ones with the thumb-prints on.

Towards midnight he braved the lift and slipped down to the ground floor in Madame Grante's dressing-gown in order to rescue the bird cage. Luckily it was still where he had left it. After that he spent a fruitless hour trying to catch JoJo, but JoJo wasn't having any. He was a past-master at the art of allowing his adversary to get within a few centimetres of touching distance, before flying off. If it happened once, it happened a hundred times. In the end, worn out by all the exertion, Monsieur Pamplemousse gave it up as a bad job, tied the cage door open with a piece of string, and lay back on Madame Grante's bed.

He stared up at the ceiling, contemplating his lot. There had to be better ways of spending an evening in Paris. Correction: there undoubtedly *were* better ways of spending an evening in Paris. Thousands of them.

He ran his eye along a row of books on a shelf in the bedside cabinet. The selection was no more exciting than it had been in the other room. He was in no mood for anything deep. Idly he removed a copy of the green Michelin *Guide de Tourisme* for the Jura. It was a recent edition. Presumably Madame Grante had acquired it when she went on her ill-fated holiday.

A folded brochure marked the town of Belfort.

Some three pages of the guide were devoted to its history and its *Curiosités*, of which there appeared to be a good many, including a statue of a giant lion eleven metres high and twenty-two metres long, carved by Bartholdi to celebrate the heroism of the town's population in defending it against the onslaught of forty thousand Germans during the siege of 1870. Situated as it was in the gap between the Vosges and the Jura Mountains it was a natural route for any invaders from the east. Its defence by Colonel Denfert-Rochereau – he who not only had an *avenue* and a *place* named after him in the capital, but also the Métro station nearest to the Catacombs – was one of the few glorious episodes of the Franco-Prussian war. Earlier still, Vauban, whose statue was not a stone's throw from *Le Guide*'s offices, had built the fortifications, from the terrace of which there was one of those *beaux panoramas* so beloved by Michelin. The Square E.-Lechten boasted a *grande variété de plantes et de fleurs*. Perhaps it was there that Madame Grante had met her *paramour*.

The river Savoureuse flowed through the town. The Canal de Montbéliard to the east joined up with the Canal du Rhône au Rhin. To the west the A36 *autoroute* provided a link between Germany and Switzerland on the one hand and central France on the other. Perhaps not surprisingly, those factors together with its situation had been of considerable economic importance to Belfort in recent years.

He turned to the brochure. There were pictures of the lion and of the old city, with its views of the river and the surrounding mountains. Another page was devoted to the industrial area which had grown up in the eastern half of the town, turning it into a centre for many enterprises ranging from metallurgy to textiles, through plastics, to locomotives and electronic equipment. Honeywell-Bull had a factory there.

Monsieur Pamplemousse sat up in bed with a start, suddenly wide awake. Was he about to establish yet another external connection?

He picked up the telephone and dialled Mademoiselle Borel's number. It was answered almost immediately.

'Martine, forgive me, I wouldn't do this normally, but it is urgent.'

Despite the lateness of the hour, she didn't seem at all put out. 'I have been trying to get you. No one seemed to know where you were.'

'Tell me?'

'No, you first.'

Monsieur Pamplemousse took a deep breath. He was only too aware that the question uppermost in his mind could well have been answered by a simple call to the telephone exchange.

'I saw in your c.v. that you had a spell with Honeywell-Bull. Was it in Belfort?'

'No, it was at Angers. I was helping to develop a new mainframe computer system. But I have been to Belfort.' She pre-empted his next question. 'That is why I have been trying to get hold of you. The Poulanc factory is also there. I should have thought of it too. I was so pleased to have got the list of names I couldn't wait to get them to you.'

'There is no reason why you should have done. I only asked for the location of a photographer.'

'Even so.'

'It was of very great help. It narrowed the field. It also acted as a catalyst.' Briefly he told her of the conversation he'd had with the girl from the Communications Room.

'But you still don't have a name?'

'Not yet.'

'If you do, be sure and let me know. He may have a credit card and I could find out more about him.'

'That is possible?'

'I have a friend, back in the States. He has access to information through the International Association of Credit Card
Investigators in California. Strictly confidential, of course.'

'Of course.'

Monsieur Pamplemousse was wide awake by now. His
mind was racing with questions.

'The computer uses *disques, oui?*'

'If it is the model you say it is.'

'How long would it take to change the information on
one?'

'That depends. If whoever did it was able to access the
mainframe and the material was pre-prepared either on *disque*
or on tape, then very little time at all. An entire novel can be
transferred in a matter of a few minutes.'

'And if it wasn't pre-prepared? If he was making the
changes as he went along?'

'Then a very long time. Certainly no faster than a person
can type. There is also the fact that he would have had to
work at night when the computer wasn't being used. That
would have halved the available time.'

'Whoever did it went to a lot of trouble. It wasn't simply a
matter of jumbling up a few entries – he went through the
entire book making outrageous alterations. Had it ever seen
the light of day there would have been enough libel actions to
keep the lawyers busy for years. Given the fact that *Le Guide*
was still in a state of preparation and was being constantly
updated, he would have had to work extremely fast.' Monsieur Pamplemousse was thinking aloud by now, acutely
conscious that his questions were self-answering.

'Extremely.'

'We have been assuming all along that "all external connections were correct" and that the material on the print-out was
a doctored version of the forthcoming guide, but supposing it
wasn't – supposing he had simply taken the current guide and
changed that?'

'Then he would have had all the time in the world. He
could have done it at his leisure and then simply transferred
the material at the last possible moment.'

'Like the night before the launch party?'

'Exactly.'

'And to do that quickly?'

'If it was fed in electronically it doesn't matter what the information was on. It could have been on tape – a different size of *disque* . . . anything. It would simply be a matter of accessing the mainframe and feeding the signal in, erasing the original at the same time.

'If it was done manually, then provided whoever is responsible knew what they were doing and had access to the computer room it would only be a matter of seconds to make the change.'

'But for the latter the *disque* would need to be physically the same as the original?'

'Clearly, yes. And since the system is peculiar to Poulanc that would imply the use of a similar machine at some stage, which makes the source of the photograph all the more interesting.'

'What would your guess be?'

There was a pause. 'If it was just an ordinary hacker, then I would say from the outside every time. A hacker would see the whole thing as a challenge. And even if they were caught he or she might get away with it. The law has yet to catch up on the complexities of electronic breaking and entering. It isn't necessarily a criminal offence. Usually they are charged with some petty offence, like stealing electricity. From what you have told me so far . . . '

'It has become a matter of life and death.'

'In that case my guess would be that a carefully prepared *disque* was transferred physically at some point prior to the launch party. If, as you say, the copy *disque* has also been tampered with, then that could have been done at the same time, either physically or electronically. Again, my guess would be the former. It would save time.'

'So it is possible that the original and its copy are still in existence?'

'That is an area where your guess is as good as mine. He might have kept them. He might have thrown them away. It

121

would most likely be a decision of the moment. He could have been tempted to keep them as a souvenir. Something to gloat over in his old age. Or he might simply have dropped them in a litter bin.'

'What do you really think?'

'I think you would have made a very good detective.'

'*Merci*. I am sorry to have troubled you at such an ungodly hour.'

'Do not worry. I was awake anyway. Thank you for your message. I am now deeply into the wines of Bordeaux. There are so many alternatives.'

'*A bientôt*'

'Sleep well.'

Monsieur Pamplemousse replaced the receiver and lay back again.

Sleep well! It was easier said than done. His mind was racing with thoughts of one kind and another. He looked around for an alarm clock, but either Madame Grante relied on instinct or she had taken it with her for some reason. He toyed with the idea of telephoning Martine again and asking her to give him an early call, but for all he knew she might want to catch up on some sleep herself if she was still working. He decided against it. He might even spend the time reading.

Much as he hated wishing his life away, he couldn't wait for the morning. Either the note he'd left on the Director's tomb would produce results or it wouldn't. If it didn't? If it didn't, then perhaps he would have to go to the Director and admit defeat, hand over all he knew to the police and let them get on with it. It would go against the grain, but at least he would have done his best and it would absolve him of the responsibility if anything went wrong. Two days had gone by; two to go. The sands of time were running out.

He woke once in the night to the sound of Pommes Frites stirring. Luckily he had left JoJo shut up in the living-room, otherwise he might have suspected the worst. With that thought uppermost in his mind he went straight back to sleep again.

When Monsieur Pamplemousse woke the sun was stream-ing in through chinks in the shutters. The sky was as clear as though it had never rained before or ever would again. Windows were open all around him. People were emerging as though from a long sleep. He was about to fling open his own windows when he remembered JoJo.

He looked at his watch. It was just gone eight thirty. There was no need to hurry. Time enough for a leisurely bath, a shave, then breakfast with the toasted remains of the *baguette* before he got dressed.

His frugal breakfast over, he found an electric iron in one cupboard and an ironing-board in another. He looked at his watch again. It was already nine fifteen. His ablutions had been perhaps a trifle too leisurely. Time was no longer on his side.

One bright spot was that JoJo had gone back into the cage of his own accord. Monsieur Pamplemousse hastily shut the door. Perhaps it was a good omen. At least it was one problem out of the way.

Opening the doors to the balcony he went outside to get his clothes and then stopped dead in his tracks.

Even sensitive to certain 'key' words, like '*Sacrebleu*' '*Nom de nom*' and '*Morbleu*', to name but a brief selection of those which reached his ears from the balcony on the present occasion, Pommes Frites came rushing out to see what was happening. As he skidded to a halt alongside his master he, too, looked as though he could hardly believe his eyes. His jaw dropped and he gave vent to a loud howl. For, as with the Emperor in Hans Andersen's immortal tale, Monsieur Pamplemousse's clothes were conspicuous by their absence. All he had left in the world were the shoes he stood up in.

'*Sacrebleu! Nom de nom! Morbleu!*'

Monsieur Pamplemousse gave a start as he heard a small voice repeating his words somewhere inside the apartment. Trust Madame Grante to have a *oiseau* that was quick on the uptake.

'*Sacrebleu! Nom de nom! Morbleu!*'

It was like having a child who inevitably gravitates towards the one word you don't want it to repeat. Even Pommes Frites looked impressed.

'*Sacrebleu! Nom de nom! Morbleu!*'

'*Sacrebleu! Nom de nom! Morbleu!*'

In contemplating his lot, Monsieur Pamplemousse couldn't but feel that a profane *oiseau* – particularly one which belonged to Madame Grante – was all he needed to make his cup of unhappiness, already not far short of the brim, full to overflowing.

Given all the circumstances, for Monsieur Pamplemousse to have arrived outside Aux Deux Magots some five minutes ahead of time was little short of a miracle. The hands of the clock on the bell tower of the church of Saint-Germain-des-Prés showed 09.55 as he arrived in the *Place*. Panic had lent him speed. He had practically run the last few hundred metres from the Odéon Métro station, taking a circuitous route which kept him clear of the crowds in the Boulevard Saint-Germain itself, which was probably just as well in the circumstances. Apart from a brief, but nonetheless unpleasant encounter with a leering *clochard* at Châtelet who refused to take '*non*' for an answer, the journey had been mercifully without incident; most of those out and about had other things on their mind. All the same, he was thankful to have made it.

He was followed into the Place Saint-Germain-des-Prés at approximately 09.55 plus fifteen seconds by Pommes Frites, pointedly keeping his distance.

A dress which was patently too small by several sizes revealed parts of Monsieur Pamplemousse which, in Pommes Frites' humble opinion, would have been best kept to himself rather than shared with those passers-by who chose to take a second, and sometimes even a third, look. A student of fashion might well have had a few things to say on the subject of matching shoes, a Hermes representative would have looked askance at the way in which one of their scarves had been tightly knotted across the lower half of the face rather than draped loosely round the neck or over the head; a milliner would have thrown up his hands in disgust; Pierre Cardin, whilst applauding the choice of sun-glasses bearing his name, might have pointed out that in designing them he'd had in mind a Mediterranean beach in high summer rather than Paris in March.

Their views would have found a ready and willing listener in Monsieur Pamplemousse. Had he decided to take up a new career as a drag artist, Madame Grante's wardrobe would not have been his first choice; it wouldn't even have made the short list. But beggars could not be choosers, and he'd had no option.

Pommes Frites' reason for keeping his distance was much more basic. Although he had become accustomed over the years to his master's vagaries, he knew that others were not always quite so tolerant. He had no wish to be seen by any of his friends in the unlikely event of their straying across the river onto the Left Bank.

It was largely the presence of such thoughts that made him linger on the corner of the Place Saint-Germain-des-Prés and the Rue de l'Abbaye while he made up his mind what to do next, whether to follow his master into the café or wait for him outside.

As Pommes Frites stood weighing up the pros and cons of the situation he became aware of an unusual scent, one with which he had become all too familiar over the past few days. He was too well trained to react, as some dogs might have done, by seeking out the source as a matter of urgency. Instead, he remained exactly where he was. The only outward signs of anything untoward were the faintest twitching of his nostrils and a certain restlessness in the way his tail flicked to and fro, as though engaged in seeing off a swarm of unseasonable flies. After a moment or two, even those manifestations of unease died away as he mentally homed in on a nearby shop, and then more specifically on the figure of a man lurking in the doorway with his back towards the street.

Whilst gazing casually about him, Pommes Frites also noted an unusually strong police presence in and around the area. There was a blue van parked a little way along the road and two more were blocking the Rue Guillaume-Apollinaire on the far side; all were full of men in uniform. Several police motor cycles were parked in the Boulevard Saint-Germain, their riders astride them, ready to go into action at a moment's notice. Two more policemen were directing the traffic. Another was addressing a walkie-talkie.

The information having been duly recorded, Pommes Frites decided to stay put for the time being and await further developments.

Unaware of Pommes Frites' thought processes at that precise moment, Monsieur Pamplemousse opened a current copy of *Le Guide* which he had borrowed from Madame Grante, turned to page 221, then entered Aux Deux Magots through the centre door opposite the *Place*. Pointedly flourishing the book aloft for all to see, he looked around for a vacant seat in the terrace section. His heart sank. For a start, he hadn't pictured it still being enclosed for the winter, and despite the comparatively early hour, it was already full to overflowing. Usually by that time in the year people would be sitting outside as well.

Looking very aggrieved, Monsieur Pamplemousse set off down the narrow central aisle, weaving his way in and out of the tables and wickerwork chairs in a crab-like motion. It would be a disastrous twist of fate if after all the trouble he had been to he couldn't find anywhere to sit. As he neared a table in the far corner he spotted an empty chair. It would afford him an ideal position from which he could keep an eye on things without being overlooked from behind. An elderly American couple about to start their breakfast eyed him nervously as he drew near.

Desperate situations called for desperate measures. '*S'il vous plaît?*' Before they had a chance to reply, Monsieur Pamplemousse was sitting alongside them. Pursing his heavily painted lips, he bestowed a beatific smile in their direction whilst helping himself to one of their *croissants*.

'*Merci!*'

As the couple hastily gathered up their belongings and fled the table, Monsieur Pamplemousse put his handbag firmly down on one of the vacant chairs and his guide on the other, daring anyone else to join him.

Smothering any feelings of guilt he might normally have had at inflicting such a grievous wound to Franco-American relations, he settled himself down and looked for a waiter. There wasn't one to be seen. He wondered if the *café* still came in two-cup size pots borne on a silver tray. It was a long time since he had last been there. The previous occupants of the table had been about to drink *chocolat* – the cup nearest to him was still hot. He took a quick sip. It tasted deliciously rich and warming.

Outside in the *Place* the tree buds were at bursting point. The cobbled paving was still damp from its morning wash. A 39 *autobus* went past, heading towards the Seine. For some reason best known to themselves all the passengers were looking out of the window and pointing towards the café.

He glanced around. In the old days the bills had been stamped *Le rendez-vous de l'élite intellectuelle*. Perhaps they still were, although nothing was for ever. Most of the present clientele could hardly be described as intellectual, let alone *élite*. If he met any of them on a dark night he would give them a wide berth. Even through his dark glasses they looked sordid enough to make the most unwashed of intellectuals appear positively angelic. Jean-Paul Sartre would turn in his grave if he saw the depths to which one of his favourite haunts had sunk; Simone de Beauvoir would have walked out, never to return. What was the world coming to? He hadn't seen such a motley collection of riff-raff since his days on the beat. The lower slopes of Montmartre at five o'clock in the morning could hardly have thrown up a more unsavoury assortment of humanity.

Monsieur Pamplemousse gave a start as he took a closer look at the occupants of the other tables. Several factors impinged on his brain at the same time. Not only was the bulk of the clientele at Aux Deux Magots that morning decidedly odd, it was also – apart from a sprinkling of unhappy-looking tourists – almost completely male; if 'male' was the right word to use. Worse still, they were all clutching open copies of *Le Guide*!

'*Merde*!' There was no need for him to waste time straining his eyes to read the page number of the one nearest to him; he knew the answer without looking. The contents of his note must have circulated like wildfire to have brought such dregs of humanity crawling out of the woodwork and from under their stones. He looked at his watch. It was almost ten o'clock exactly. Even if his quarry had intended being there he must have been frightened away by now.

Monsieur Pamplemousse had barely registered the fact when his ears were assailed by the strident blast of a whistle from somewhere close at hand. Seconds later pandemonium broke out as a horde of blue-uniformed figures suddenly appeared from nowhere and began streaming in through the door. Others appeared as if by magic to bar the exit through the main café itself.

Monsieur Pamplemousse's first regret was that he'd chosen a table in a corner from which there was patently no chance whatsoever of escape. His second regret was that Madame Grante's handbag was full to overflowing with his own belongings. He looked in vain for somewhere to hide his copy of *Le Guide*.

'*Monsieur* . . . ' A stocky figure clad in a black leather jacket and riot gear appeared in front of him and held out his hand. 'May I see that?'

Monsieur Pamplemousse did a quick flick of his wrist. 'Of course, *Monsieur*. I was planning a little holiday in Brittany. You will find it somewhere near the beginning of the book.'

Looking him straight in the eye the man turned the pages back again.

'I think you have made a mistake, *Monsieur*. On page 221 you are in the Jura.'

Monsieur Pamplemousse gave up. It had been worth a try, but there was no point in arguing. It was a no-win situation. He was dealing with a member of the CRS – the *Compagnie Républicaine de Sécurité*. Purposely kept caged up behind barred windows for hours on end beforehand, like a bull getting up steam before entering the ring, the man would be spoiling for a fight. One more word and it would be a charge of resisting arrest. Two and it would be a clout around the *tête* with a baton.

As he found himself being bundled unceremoniously up the steps of a waiting van along with the other occupants of the terrace, Monsieur Pamplemousse looked around for Pommes Frites. A judiciously well-placed bite on the rear of his captor would not have come amiss, but he looked in vain. For once his friend was nowhere to be seen.

Although not visible to Monsieur Pamplemousse, Pommes Frites was, in fact, quite near at hand. He was caught on the horns of a dilemma. On the one hand loyalty to his master tugged him in one direction. On the other hand, all his training led him to the inescapable conclusion that he should hang on at all costs to the trail he had just picked up. He opted for the latter.

It was a difficult moment for Pommes Frites and he had the grace to avert his eyes as he saw his master being escorted from Aux Deux Magots before disappearing behind the crowd that had already collected outside, avid as ever for a free spectacle, just as they had been centuries before when on that very same spot justice had been dispensed on the gibbet and pillory by those in power.

Fortunately, looking the other way gave him a great advantage, for he was just in time to see his quarry boarding an *autobus*.

Without a moment's hesitation, he set off in pursuit. The antique shops of the Rue Bonaparte, the view from the Pont du Carrousel, the glass pyramid covering the new entrance hall of the Louvre, all passed in a flash as he strove to keep up with the *autobus* while it crossed the Rue de Rivoli and thence into the Place Palais-Royal. So intent was he on his task that when it pulled up at the first stop in the Avenue de l'Opéra he overtook it and nearly missed seeing the man get off. He was now waiting in the shelter, looking back the way he had come. Following a zig-zag course, sniffing at various objects *en route*, Pommes Frites retraced his steps and then stationed himself on the other side of the glass where he could keep a watchful eye on the man's legs.

Several more *autobus* went past before the other made a move. Then, as the fourth one arrived, he climbed on. Pommes Frites sprang into action again, following on behind as it turned right into the Rue Sainte-Anne. This time the going was much easier, for the road was narrow and progress was slow. The problem was not so much one of keeping up with the *autobus*, but occupying himself inconspicuously while it squeezed its way in between various lorries and road-works *en route*. In the end Pommes Frites decided to keep as far behind it as possible, hoping he wouldn't be seen. He was glad that he had, for as the *autobus* made another right turn, this time into the much wider Rue du Quatre Septembre, it came to a halt again and he saw the man get off, hesitate for a moment or two, then take shelter in a nearby doorway.

As though engaged on an important errand, Pommes Frites turned left, then paused to relieve himself on the nearside wheel of a large *camion* parked at the side of the road. He positioned himself so that he would get a good look at his quarry, imprinting the image on his memory for future reference.

It was as well that he did, for he had scarcely begun to tap his ample reserves when another *autobus* drew up and he saw the man break cover and move towards it. Once again luck was with Pommes Frites: it was an *autobus* with an open rear platform. He was over the rail in a flash. The driver was too busy watching the traffic as he pulled out to notice, and if anyone else did they failed to react.

The journey this time was much longer and Pommes Frites was beginning to wonder if he'd been given the slip when, through a gap between the side and a handrail, he saw the man getting off again.

Pommes Frites waited until he was looking the other way and then, as the *autobus* stopped at some traffic lights a little further on, he seized his opportunity. He was just in time to see the man disappearing down a side-street. Hastily marking the spot in the time-honoured way that nature had intended,

Pommes Frites followed on behind at a respectable distance. As he did so he sniffed the air, his brain cells beginning to work overtime as he weighed up the pros and cons of the situation.

Although relatively unversed in the thought processes which had gone into the planning of the Paris *autobus* system, he was all too conscious that if his sense of smell hadn't let him down and he was where he thought he was, then there had to be quicker ways of reaching it than the route they had taken. All of which led him to but one conclusion: the man he had been following didn't want to be followed, and if that was the case then in Pommes Frites' view, it was a very good reason for doing just that.

Having reached that decision, Pommes Frites quickened his pace, the smell of stagnant water growing stronger with every step he took.

The drive from the police station to the offices of *Le Guide* was not the happiest Monsieur Pamplemousse had ever experienced. Despite his garb, which had not improved with the passage of time, he would have preferred taking an *autobus* to riding in the Director's car. Optional extras in the way of tinted glass rendered the atmosphere even chillier than it might otherwise have been.

Monsieur Pamplemousse was the first to speak.

'It was kind of you to bail me out, *Monsieur*.'

'Frankly, Pamplemousse, kindness did not enter into the matter. The plain fact is we need you. Although, having said that, you may well be a master, or perhaps judging from your attire, *mistress* of disguise, but I fear that if nothing is forth-coming very soon, we shall have to bring in the police after all.'

Having exhausted the subject as a topic of conversation, they sat in silence for a while.

The whole episode had been a disaster. The only good thing was the fact that Amandier had been in charge of the police operation. He was one of the 'old school'. His hand-shake had been acquired many moons ago from the *gendarmerie*'s standard book of etiquette, 'Advice from an Old to a Young Gendarme', and it showed. If it had been one of the younger ones who knew him only by reputation he wouldn't have fancied his chances. He would still be languishing in the cells along with the others. It was one of those occasions when the French legal system which decreed your being guilty until you managed to prove otherwise had its drawbacks. Proof of his innocence, whatever the charges, would have taken for ever. At least no one had thought of comparing his handwriting with that on the note in the Père-Lachaise. It would have been hard to talk his way out of that one.

It was the Director's turn to break the silence.

'The computer threw up an interesting fact this morning,' he began, apropos of nothing, as they turned into the Rue du Bac. 'Overnight, sales of last year's copies of *Le Guide* have risen phenomenally. Orders have been flooding in. It points to a great upsurge in our popularity.'

'Did the computer also throw up where the sales took place, *Monsieur?*'

'Strangely enough, they were all in Paris – mostly in the twentieth *arrondissement*. It seems that local bookstores there have sold out and demand has since spread to the surrounding areas. Brentano's in the Avenue de l'Opéra were in a state of siege yesterday evening and again early this morning. If the trend continues nationwide, and *if* next year's edition is ever published, we shall need to treble our print order. The projected sales graph is already off the board. I have ordered an extension.'

'I think I would hold your hand, *Monsieur.*'

The Director swerved violently and under the pretext of avoiding an oncoming *camion*, edged nearer the offside window. 'I'd rather you didn't, Pamplemousse!' he exclaimed. 'In fact, I would go so far as to suggest that after all this is over you should seek medical advice. You may be in need of a rest. A spell by the sea may not come amiss. You can have the use of my summer residence in Normandy if you wish. The cold wind blowing in from *La Manche* often works wonders.'

Monsieur Pamplemousse heaved a sigh. 'You think I should wait that long, *Monsieur?*'

His sarcasm was wasted.

'Much as it grieves me to say so, Pamplemousse, we cannot spare you at this particular time for such luxuries. It will have to wait. Every moment counts.'

'You misunderstand me, *Monsieur.*' As briefly as possible, Monsieur Pamplemousse outlined the reason for his being in Aux Deux Magots. From there it was but a short step to the possible reason behind the increase in sales. The Director listened in silence.

'I find this incredible, Pamplemousse. Did you give no thought at all to the plight of any poor innocent tourists caught up in your goings-on, had they happened to be carrying a copy of *Le Guide* as so many of them do?

'The repercussions have already begun. The American Embassy has registered a protest in the strongest possible terms. The police did not stop with those on the terrace. All the occupants of the café were removed for questioning; passers-by were arrested on suspicion.'

'They were quite safe, *Monsieur*, provided their copy of *Le Guide* was not open at page 221.'

'Humph.' The Director gave his passenger an odd look, then drove in silence for a while, clearly lost in thought.

'Between you, me and the *montant de barrière*, Pamplemousse,' he said at last, 'there are moments when I begin to wonder if I made the right decision in committing our entire future to an electronic chip. Management can all too easily become divorced from the assets it is supposed to be managing. The sales figures are another case in point. A snap decision based on the computer's findings would have been disastrous.'

'A computer is only as good as the information fed into it, *Monsieur*. It cannot work miracles. However, assuming all external connections are correct . . . ' Almost without thinking, Monsieur Pamplemousse found himself quoting Mademoiselle Borel.

The Director listened with half an ear as he negotiated the

stream of traffic converging on the Esplanade des Invalides. He stopped at the entrance to *Le Guide* in order to show his pass, watched with distaste while Monsieur Pamplemousse rummaged in Madame Grante's handbag before doing likewise, then drove round the fountain in the middle of the inner courtyard before coming to rest, not in his usual marked parking area to the right of the main entrance, but alongside a small service door some way beyond it. He withdrew a plastic entry card from his wallet and was about to hand it to Monsieur Pamplemousse when he paused. He suddenly looked tired and dispirited.

'*Comment ça va*, Aristide?'

'*Comment ça va?*' Monsieur Pamplemousse gave a shrug. What was there to say? Everything and nothing.

'You are pursuing your enquiries?'

'I have not been idle. I think I may have found out *how* it was done. I have yet to find out why, or indeed the name of the person responsible. To do that I may have to visit Belfort.'

For some reason his words had a strange effect on the Director. He went pale and for a brief moment seemed almost to shrink inside himself.

Monsieur Pamplemousse looked at him with some concern. 'Is anything the matter, *Monsieur*? Can I get you some water?'

'*Eau?*' The very thought seemed to bring about a miraculous recovery. 'If what I suspect is true, Pamplemousse, it will need something far stronger than *eau* to set matters right!

'If you will excuse me, I will just park the car. You carry on up and I will see you in my office. Before we go any further there are things I feel I should tell you.'

8

CONFESSION TIME

Monsieur Pamplemousse rose to his feet as the Director entered the office. He received a peremptory wave in return, indicating that he should return to his seat.

'Brace yourself, Pamplemousse.' The Director stationed himself behind his desk. 'I fear I have bad news.'

'*Monsieur?*'

'Pamplemousse, an attempt has been made on the life of the *oiseau!*'

'JoJo?' If the Director had announced that someone had planted a bomb under his chair, Monsieur Pamplemousse could hardly have been more surprised. It was the last thing he'd expected to hear. He glanced round automatically towards the table where he had last seen the bird cage. It was now shrouded in a dark green cloth.

'He is not . . . ?'

'Fortunately, no. Although he is still in a state of shock. I must confess I keep the house covered with a cloth because I cannot stand constant chirruping in the mornings.'

'*Alors?*'

'At oh, eight twenty-five this morning, Pamplemousse, shortly before I arrived at the office, a man purporting to be a veterinary surgeon called to take him away. He was allowed as far as reception and the cage was brought down. Fortunately, thanks to the vigilance of the gatekeeper, the attempt was forestalled. Rambaud came on duty just as the man was about to leave. Having overheard our conversation the day before, and knowing the importance we attach to the *oiseau's* well-being, he asked to see the man's credentials. When he couldn't produce them Rambaud refused to release the cage and threatened to call the police. After a brief tug-of-war – during which, I regret to say, the bars of the *oiseau*'s cage were nearly torn asunder, the would-be assassin made off. As he did so Rambaud heard him utter the ominous word *"Vendredi"*. Today, I need hardly remind you, Pamplemousse, is Thursday. You have one day left.'

Monsieur Pamplemousse considered the matter. He couldn't help feeling that the Director's interpretation of the event verged on the over-dramatic. Trying to remove JoJo from the office hardly came under the heading of attempted murder, but doubtless his chief was beginning to feel the strain. All the same, it was certainly very strange, particularly in view of the feeling he'd had the previous evening that someone had been in Madame Grante's apartment. Perhaps whoever it was had gone there first looking for JoJo and drawn a blank. If they had then tried at the office it could mean only one thing. His own movements must have been under close scrutiny, which was disconcerting to say the least.

As Monsieur Pamplemousse sat down heavily in the visitor's chair a pained expression came over the Director's face.

'Aristide, I do wish you would either cross your legs or sit facing the other way. I find the view from my desk somewhat disconcerting.'

'*Pardon, Monsieur.*' Monsieur Pamplemousse became aware of a faint tearing sound as he struggled to reach a suitable compromise half-way between comfort and decorum. It was a simple case of trying unsuccessfully to get a generous litre into a bare demi-litre *pot*. Something went 'twang'.

'*Merde!*' It was too late, the damage had been done. He rubbed his right thigh.

'A woman's life is full of problems, *Monsieur*, not the least of which I have discovered is how to sit down gracefully without revealing that for but one glimpse of which many men would give their eye-teeth.'

'I bow to your superior knowledge, Pamplemousse,' said

the Director severely. 'However, most women are more cir-
cumspect when it comes to shopping for their nether gar-
ments.'

'These came from a little *boutique* in the Rue Cler,
Monsieur . . . '

'I have no wish to know where you bought them, Pamplemousse. They make you look like an advertisement for a
house of ill repute. One which has all too clearly seen better
days, if I may say so.'

'I did not buy them, *Monsieur*. They belong to Madame
Grante . . . '

The Director gave a start. 'Madame Grante!' Sitting bolt
upright, he took a closer look. 'Who would have thought it,
Aristide? Women are strange creatures, they really are. A
different breed. How can a mere male ever really be expected
to know what goes on inside their minds? I know the shop
very well. Brevity is often combined, it seems to me, with
untold complexity. I invariably hurry past.'

'In the words of the song, *Monsieur*, love is a tender trap.
Madame Grante must have been hit very hard.'

'Yes, yes.' A look of impatience crossed the Director's face
as yet another tearing sound emerged from the depths of the
chair.

'Pamplemousse, I have a spare suit in the bedroom next
door. It is kept there for emergencies. Before we go any
further, I suggest you make use of it. You will find it very
much on the tight side, I fear, but it will be an improvement
on your present mode of dress. There are also some shirts in
one of the drawers.'

Monsieur Pamplemousse was only too willing to oblige.
He had no wish to stay looking the way he was for a second
longer than necessary. He also sensed that the Director
needed a little time in which to gather his thoughts. He had
mentioned having more than one matter he wished to talk
about. Clearly, from the nervous way he was drumming on
his desk, there was something other than the attempted
abduction of JoJo on his mind.

While he was exchanging his chemise for a snow-white

shirt bearing the Charvet label, Monsieur Pamplemousse's thoughts gravitated towards Pommes Frites. It was unlike him to go off on his own for so long. On the other hand, he was well able to look after himself and at least he was on home ground. Pommes Frites knew his way around Paris better than most humans – guidebooks were an unnecessary luxury. All the same, he couldn't help wondering what was keeping him.

The socks and tie were from Marcel Lassance.

The Director had been doing his wardrobe less than justice. There was not one suit hanging on a rail, but several. Monsieur Pamplemousse chose one of medium blue with a discreet pin-stripe. It fitted him like a glove. He looked at the label inside the jacket. It was by André Bardot. Considering his reflection in a full-length mirror, he found himself looking at a stranger; Doucette would hardly have recognised him. Removing a speck of invisible dust from one of the lapels, he closed the cupboard door and went back into the office.

The Director was standing at the window perusing an old copy of *Le Guide*.

He looked round anxiously as Monsieur Pamplemousse entered. 'Mind how you sit!' he exclaimed. 'I don't wish to hear any more untoward noises.'

Monsieur Pamplemousse lowered himself carefully into the chair and then draped one leg elegantly over the other. 'There is no cause for alarm, *Monsieur*. The suit is a perfect fit. It could have been made for me. I am most grateful.'

'Hmmm.' The Director looked less than pleased at the news as he turned his attention to the book he was holding aloft.

'Pamplemousse, you mentioned a certain word to me just now.'

'I am sorry, *Monsieur*. I'm afraid it slipped out.'

'No, no, Pamplemousse.' The Director clucked impatiently. 'I was not referring to your earlier use of an expletive, rather to something you said when we arrived. You used the word "Belfort". It confirmed my worst suspicions.'

'It did, *Monsieur*?'

'Pamplemousse, tell me what you know about *poulets de Bresse.*'

Monsieur Pamplemousse heaved an inward sigh. He had lost track of the date, but he must be coming up to his annual salary review. At such times the Director had a habit of shooting odd questions at members of staff under the guise of pretending he wanted the information for some new project. Usually it was on a subject he had only recently looked up. It was a kind of oral test paper, replacing the conventional interview.

He closed his eyes in order to concentrate his thoughts. He was getting off lightly. Everyone knew about *poulets de Bresse*, famous for centuries as the best chicken in the world.

'They are, of course, from the plain of Bresse – Brillat-Savarin country, and birthplace of Fernand Point – but more particularly from an area within the plain amounting to some 400 square kilometres – an area which was first defined as long ago as 1936. Within that area seven breeders supply day-old chicks to a thousand or so farmers, each of whom may raise a maximum of five hundred birds at a time – in other words a grand total of not more than half a million a year. The birds spend thirty-five days as chicks and then they are allowed outside to run freely on the grass, each one being allotted a minimum area of ten square metres – which is a good deal more than the average Parisian enjoys. During that time they are fed on cereals – mostly corn – and skimmed milk. At fourteen weeks they are brought inside again for fattening until at sixteen weeks they are pronounced ready for the market. The weight of each bird before and after dressing is clearly laid down. In the latter case, no bird may go to market unless it weighs at least 1.5kg and is unblemished. A true native species of Bresse chicken has white flesh and feathers, and bluish-grey legs with four toes and a red wattle and comb. In the market itself they are clearly recognisable by a lead ring around the foot attesting to the bird's origin. Strictly speaking it should be *poularde de Bresse*, for the hen is considered much tastier than the cock. They have an unmistakable delicate flavour and they are at their best when roasted simply in a very hot oven until they are golden brown and the skin is crisp. Since 1957 they have been *Appellation d'Origine Contrôlée* and any variation on the stipulations I have mentioned is strictly against the law and a punishable offence.'

'*Exactement!*' The Director sounded so much like a schoolmaster congratulating his star pupil on passing the daily test with flying colours, Monsieur Pamplemousse felt tempted to ask if he could have the rest of the day off, but clearly it was no time for levity; there was more to come. He waited patiently.

'Have you any firsthand knowledge, Aristide, of what that punishment is?'

'A heavy fine, I would imagine, *Monsieur*. Possibly, in extreme cases, a prison sentence. If the rules are administered as strictly as those which apply to wine, and doubtless they are, then there will be very little room for manoeuvre; every factor, every process, every detail from the moment of birth will be strictly enforced.'

'And what of those on the other side of the fence? What of those who sell a *poularde* which purports to be from Bresse, but is in fact an impostor?'

'Ah, that is a different matter, *Monsieur*, but they would still find themselves in trouble. That would be a matter of fraud – of "passing off". The proper authorities would deal with the problem.'

There had been a time in Monsieur Pamplemousse's own career when he had been part of the then 200-strong section of the Paris police who served as food inspectors – that had been a major reason for his becoming interested in the whole business of *cuisine* in the first place. Then it had been a matter of checking scales for accuracy, ensuring that *croissants au beurre* contained no margarine, sampling truffled *foie gras* to make certain it contained the real thing and not the cheaper Moroccan whites dyed black; the list of their duties had been endless and they had not been the most popular members of the force.

The Director sat down at his desk again and placed the

Guide in front of him. He gazed at it for a moment or two, then spread his hands out the blotter, palms down.

'Some twenty-five years ago, Aristide, I was just one of the team. I had not long been with *Le Guide* and I was serving my apprenticeship as an Inspector. Our founder,' he turned and paid his respects to the freshly scrubbed portrait of Monsieur Hippolyte Duval, 'our founder believed in starting at the bottom, just as he had done himself many years before.

'One evening I found myself sitting in a restaurant about to tackle a *Poularde de Bresse en Vessie* – a dish for which I had a particular fancy at the time, and which was supposed to be one of their specialities. I had ordered it in advance an hour or two before my arrival. *Poularde de Bresse en Vessie*, as you know, consists of a Bresse chicken stuffed with its own liver and a little *foie gras* and some slices of truffle, poached very gently in a pig's bladder containing also carrots and leeks . . . '

Monsieur Pamplemousse knew it only too well, for it was just such a dish that had been the cause of one of his earlier adventures.

'The owner of the establishment was a brilliant up-and-coming young chef with an assured future. He had inherited the restaurant from his father, who had died earlier that same year. At the time of his father's death it rated two Stock Pots in *Le Guide* and two rosettes in Michelin – Gault-Millau didn't exist in those days – and it was heading for a third award in both. Naturally, on the death of the father, even though to all intents and purposes his son had been in charge for several years, all accolades were withdrawn. The purpose of my visit was to make a preliminary report prior to their reinstatement. At that time there was no doubt in anyone's mind that it was a mere formality, but it wasn't to work out that way.

'I knew from the moment I entered the restaurant that all was not well; there was a certain "atmosphere". The first course, *feuilleté d'asperges*, was beyond reproach, but the *maître d'hôtel* – one of the old school – was clearly ill at ease. Having presented the *poularde* to me on a silver dish, he then withdrew to a dark corner of the restaurant for it to be opened up and served, for it was still encased in its *vessie*. I can still see the pained expression on his face as he returned to my table some minutes later and placed the plate before me.

'The reason for his behaviour became all too clear the moment I took the first mouthful.

'To cut a long story short, Aristide, far from being made with a *poularde de Bresse*, the dish clearly contained a bird of the very worst kind; a cock which must have been obtained at short notice from the local *supermarché*.

'Imagine my dilemma. There I was, young and relatively inexperienced, undergoing my first real baptism of fire; not only was my own future at stake, but also the reputation of *Le Guide*. However, I had to be very sure of my facts. It is one thing making an accusation when you have proof positive – which I would have done had I seen the bird prior to its immersion in the broth. It is quite another matter when you are putting your taste-buds on the line. I took courage in a kind of sixth sense and in the end it didn't let me down.

'All the same, I have to tell you, Aristide, that when I asked to see the chef my heart was in my boots. I knew then something of what it must have been like "going over the top" in the first Great War. Heads throughout the restaurant were turned in my direction.

'It was not a pleasant experience. At first the chef tried to bluster his way out of it. He told me I didn't know what I was talking about – but his very manner betrayed his guilt. Then he offered me another dish. Finally he tore up my bill and asked me to leave the restaurant before turning on his heels and marching back to the kitchen.

'When I followed him in there and revealed the true purpose of my visit he became a changed man. First he pleaded that it had all been an unfortunate mistake – he tried to put the blame on one of the young *sous-chefs*. Then, when he saw he wasn't getting anywhere, he attempted the final insult. He took me to one side and offered a considerable sum of money if I would go away and forget the whole thing. It was at that moment that I knew I was right. I told him that my report would be submitted that very evening.

'As I uttered the words something seemed to snap. He picked up a knife – a fearsome weapon – a Sabatier *grand couteau de cuisine* with a 35cm blade – sharp as a razor – and threatened to kill me. As he advanced across the *cuisine* he removed a hair from his head and sliced it in two by way of demonstrating what he would do to parts of my anatomy before he plunged them into oil which was already boiling on the stove. He had the face of a madman, Aristide. Sweat was pouring down his face, and as he lunged at me an uncontrollable tic appeared in his right eye. For a moment or two I must confess I really did go in fear of my life. The rest of the kitchen staff had long since fled in panic, leaving me entirely on my own. Fortunately, the *maître d'hôtel* had taken it upon himself to call the police and they arrived in the nick of time.

'Two of them grabbed the man from behind, whilst a third had the presence of mind to remove the remaining tools of his trade before he was able to get his hands on them. In the ensuing struggle one of the *gendarmes* received a flesh wound. I still remember the look of naked hate on the man's face as he was led away from his restaurant, shouting and screaming and swearing revenge.

'There is no doubt in my mind that there was a screw loose somewhere, otherwise why would he have done it? There he was, a young man, just starting out in life. Granted, he had inherited the mantle of his father's success, but already he was gathering plaudits on his own account. He had no need to take short cuts or to make excuses. I can only think that false pride prevented him from saying he had run out of the real thing and, given the nature of the dish – the fact that for most of the time during its cooking the *poularde* is out of sight – he took a chance. But that doesn't excuse his action. It was an unforgivable deception.'

'What happened after that, *Monsieur?*'

'I submitted my report and in due course it was passed on to the powers that be. He suffered the usual fate. Those administering the AOC took the appropriate action. There were notices in the local *journaux*. Other notices were pasted across the window of his restaurant warning people not to patronise it. From that moment on he was ignored by his contemporaries and ostracised by the general public.

'Can you imagine what that must have meant to an up-and-coming restaurateur? No one to cook for. Above all, no one to shake hands with all day long. It would be bad enough to an ordinary Frenchman, but to the *patron* of a restaurant, it must have seemed like the end of the world.

'In due course his case came up and he was sent to prison. The restaurant struggled on for a few weeks without him, but by the time he was released it had closed down. Those in the trade made sure he was never able to work as a chef again.'

'And where was the restaurant?' Monsieur Pamplemousse knew the answer even before he posed the question.

'Need you ask, Pamplemousse? It was the very place you mentioned as we arrived. Belfort.'

'Do you remember the details, *Monsieur*?'

'They are all here, Aristide.' The Director passed the book across the table. 'The name of the restaurant and its specialities. The name of the owner. It is the edition prior to the year I made my visit. Alas, it was the last time either name appeared.'

'And there is no doubt in your mind, *Monsieur*, that the two people are one and the same?' Once again, it was a redundant question. There was no other possible explanation. The mention of the nervous tic clinched matters.

'None whatsoever. He must have been harbouring a grudge against *Le Guide* over all these years, a grudge which has been growing inside him like a cancer.'

Monsieur Pamplemousse could not but agree, with the proviso that it wasn't simply *Le Guide* against whom the man harboured a grudge, but the Director himself as the person responsible for his downfall in the first place. He glanced at the book. The entry for the restaurant had been circled in red. He copied the details into his notebook.

'It shows the kind of person we are up against, Pamplemousse.'

'*Oui, Monsieur.*'

'Clearly, he is a man who would stop at nothing. A man who would substitute a frozen bird of doubtful ancestry for a *poularde de Bresse* would be capable of anything.'

'Have you been back to Belfort since, *Monsieur*?'

'I was there several times last year in connection with the computer. On one occasion I took Madame Grante with me so that she could familiarise herself with the system. She liked the area so much she even talked of going back there for a holiday.'

'And the restaurant?'

'It is now a coin-operated dry-cleaning establishment. A sad come-down for what could have been a temple of gastronomy.'

'And do you still not wish to call in the police, *Monsieur*, even though your own life is clearly in danger?'

'No, Aristide. Now, more than ever, the answer has to be "no".'

Monsieur Pamplemousse knew better than to argue. He was aware of the signs. Once the chief had made up his mind that was that.

'May I use your telephone, *Monsieur*?'

'Go ahead, Pamplemousse.'

He rang Martine Borel's number. She answered straight away.

'The name is Dubois. He may be using something else, but I doubt it. With a name like Dubois who needs anonymity? Why make unnecessary complications?'

'Hold on a moment while I grab a pen.'

Briefly he read out the details.

'Were you serious about finding credit information?' There was a pause during which he could hear the rattle of a keyboard. 'It is not a good time of day.' She sounded hesitant. 'The person lives in California and there is a nine-hour time difference; it may take a little while, but I will do my best.' There was another brief pause. 'I have an address for him on the Minitel.'

'Marvellous.' The wonders of science! He listened as she reeled it off. 'If I am not in the office try me on . . . ' He flipped back through his notebook and gave her Madame Grante's number.

He tried dialling a second number.

Jacques was out on a case; there was no knowing when he would be back. He left the details with an underling. The man seemed less than enthusiastic.

'That is a long time ago . . . '

'Anything would be helpful. He has a record, back in . . . ' he looked at the date on the outside of *Le Guide*, '1963.

'It might be worth trying the hotels. He must have been staying somewhere.

'I'll get a photo over to you as quickly as possible.

'No, I don't know if he is still using the same name . . .

'*Oui*, I know you will have to check with Jacques . . . '

One thing was for sure, he wasn't going to end up with dinner at Les Tourelles. The way things were going it would be Taillevant or nothing.

'*Oui*, it is urgent.'

It was worth a try. At least it meant he had more than one iron in the fire.

'What do you think we should do about the *oiseau*?' asked the Director as Monsieur Pamplemousse replaced the receiver. 'It seems to have assumed some importance in the eyes of our adversary. He may well try again.'

Monsieur Pamplemousse raised his eyes heavenwards. He'd forgotten about JoJo's stand-in. 'You are right, *Monsieur*. The *oiseau* must be put in a place of safety.' It was better to go along with the idea than try to explain.

'A matter for security, would you not agree?'

'*Oui, Monsieur*.'

'*Bon*.' The Director rose to his feet and crossed to the cage. 'In that case, Pamplemousse, I suggest you take him with you. I have had the bars straightened, and clearly the *oiseau* knows something, otherwise why would the man wish to remove it? I have tried to break down the barriers of communication and failed. It is your turn now.'

'But, *Monsieur* – '

'No "buts", Pamplemousse. That is an order.'

146

'In which case, *Monsieur*, speaking as Head of Security I suggest that you remain in this building until such time as it is safe to leave.'

'Aristide, is that strictly necessary?'

'That, too, is an order, *Monsieur*. Unless, of course, you would prefer me to resign?'

The Director gave a sigh as Monsieur Pamplemousse stood up to leave. *'Touché*, Pamplemousse. But I hope it will not be for too long.'

'I hope so too, *Monsieur*.' Monsieur Pamplemousse spoke with rather more confidence than he felt.

'One last thing, Aristide . . . '

Monsieur Pamplemousse paused at the door. *'Monsieur?'*

'Don't forget the *oiseau!*'

9

POMMES FRITES TAKES THE PLUNGE

On his way back to Madame Grante's apartment Monsieur Pamplemousse called in at the Rue Poncelet and did some shopping. He bought a *baguette*, still slightly warm to the touch from the second baking of the day, and a *tarte aux fraises*. Further along the street he called in at a *charcuterie* and purchased a thick slice of *jambon*, smoked in oak from the forests of the Ardennes, and some slices of underdone Charolais beef. To this he added a generous helping of black olives and another of gherkins, ten quail's eggs, a selection of salads, a portion of Camembert Fermier – true, it was a little early in the year, the milk would not yet have reached its best quality, but unpasteurised cheese was becoming more and more difficult to find and it was hard to resist – and a portion of smooth, buttery-looking Roquefort. Laid out on the counter in front of him it added up to a simple enough repast, but it would help tide him over until he was able to order a proper meal. As an afterthought he asked for a slice of *pâté forestière* – it would go well with the gherkins. Better safe than sorry: he might have a long wait.

In truth, although he had talked to the chief about going to Belfort, there really didn't seem much point – even if he'd had the time. He now knew all he really needed to know. Paris was where the action was. If necessary he would carry on playing cat and mouse until something concrete turned up.

At an *épicerie fine*, he treated himself to a bottle of Volnay; an '80 Clos des Chênes from Michel Lafarge.

He half hoped to see Pommes Frites waiting for him outside Madame Grante's block, but the street was deserted.

As he took the lift up to her apartment for the third evening running, Monsieur Pamplemousse found himself looking out for signs of life on the other landings. Already he had established a nodding acquaintance with several of the tenants. It was amazing how quickly one was accepted with no questions asked. The saxophone player was at it again.

Once inside the apartment he set to work laying the table, but gradually his pace began to slacken, until by the time he finally drew up a chair and sat down he found he had lost his appetite. It was the kind of meal which needed company.

He poured himself a glass of Volnay instead. It was an impeccable balance of fruit and perfume, an elegant wine, but again, a wine to be shared.

And that was the truth of the matter. He suddenly felt very lonely without Pommes Frites. They would have enjoyed the evening together.

After toying in a desultory fashion with the *pâté* he tried telephoning the caretaker back at his own apartment. It was just possible that Pommes Frites might have gone home – but he drew a blank. There was no report of his having been seen for several days.

Monsieur Pamplemousse looked out of the window. The gardens at the back of the block were deserted. Lights were beginning to come on in the surrounding buildings. He drew the curtains and then turned on the television. It was '*Chiffres et Nombres*' again. It was always '*Chiffres et Nombres*'.

At least, judging from the din they were making, JoJo and his companion were enjoying it. In desperation he switched the set off.

Going through the pile of records he found an old Yves Montand selection. Half-way through '*C'est si bon*' the needle stuck. He tried the Tino Rossi again. It reminded him of his early cinema-going days when he had been courting Doucette. Tino Rossi was forever playing double roles – twin brothers – the good guy and the bad guy. He'd always worn a pencil moustache and had his hair slicked down for the latter part. They were about the only changes he'd made, but for purposes of plot it had always fooled the rest of the cast,

149

especially the girls, so that one had longed to cry out a warning.

Over the cold meats and salads he took the photograph of Madame Grante's lover from his wallet and propped it up against the bottle of wine.

Dubois. Being able to put a name to the face somehow helped bring it to life. In a way, the man wasn't unlike the characters in the Tino Rossi films. He wondered which one Madame Grante had met first of all. The good guy or the bad guy? Either way, there had been no one to shout out a warning, if indeed she would have heeded it. People in love rarely did.

Dressed one way, he could imagine that all the porter had said about Dubois was probably true; he knew the type. On the other hand, wearing his casual clothes there was nothing about the man that would have caused him to stand out in a crowd. Monsieur Pamplemousse certainly didn't hold out much hope of his being picked up simply on the off-chance of someone recognising him from the picture. In a small town, possibly. People had to go out if only to do the shopping or to eat. But in a city of over ten thousand restaurants, it was too much to ask, and Paris had more than its fair share of sleazy hotels where no questions were asked provided the bill was paid.

What he needed was a break.

It came a few minutes after ten o'clock in the form of a telephone call from Martine.

Monsieur Pamplemousse listened in silence as she reeled off a list of details. There had been no credit problems. Bills had always been paid promptly. Apart from the usual selection of odds and ends most of them were to do with eating out and paying domestic accounts: gas and electricity, local taxes. All related to the Belfort area, and all very innocuous, but he could tell from the tone of her voice that there was more to come.

In early February the pattern had changed. Bills started coming in from farther afield: Montbéliard, Clerval, Laisey, then several from Besançon, two from Dole. They were over

150

a period of several days. Some were from restaurants, but mostly they were for fuel. Whatever the reason for his journey he didn't seem to be in any particular hurry.

'Hold on a moment. I will see if I can find a map.' He remembered seeing a gazetteer in the other room.

'If it's of any help I have done that already. Montbéliard is the nearest big town south of Belfort. It is on the Canal du Rhône au Rhin. Besançon is another eighty-four kilometres or so to the south-west. Dole follows on from that. They are all on the same canal. Soon after Dole it heads north and joins the river Saône at Saint-Symphorien. North of that again it meets up with the Canal de la Marne à la Saône.'

'And on to Paris.'

'Exactly. I have checked with a friend of mine who knows about these things and he says Dubois could have taken another route via the Canal de Bourgogne. That's shorter and reckoned to be the more beautiful of the two, but the first is more modern and there are far fewer locks. One hundred and fourteen as against one hundred and eighty-nine.'

Monsieur Pamplemousse was listening with only half an ear. He could have kicked himself for not having thought of it before. All along he had been picturing his quarry holed up in some small hotel. Either that or in a rented apartment. A boat was the obvious answer. The picture of him dressed in sailing gear should have provided the clue; the porter's mention of rope-soled shoes another.

'I'm sorry I can't be of any more help.'

'You have done more than enough.'

'*Bonne chance.*'

'*Merci.*'

After he had replaced the receiver Monsieur Pamplemousse lay back and thought for a while. If Dubois had set out to travel from Belfort via the Marne, then he would have arrived in Paris to the east of the city. The chances were that he would either have tied up in some backwater outside the limits – in which case the boat could be anywhere – or he might have taken it as far into Paris as it was allowed. Of the two alternatives, that seemed far more likely. In which case, entering from the east, the logical place to aim for would be the Paris-Arsenal Marina where the Canal Saint-Martin joined the Seine. That would offer a choice of escape routes if things went wrong: either back the way he had come, or on down the Seine towards Rouen and Le Havre. Failing that, he could always head northwards up the Canal Saint-Martin *en route* to Belgium and beyond.

On the other hand, if that were the case – if he had ended up in the Arsenal basin – he wouldn't be able to go anywhere without passing through a lock. There was one between the Marina and the Seine and a whole series in the Canal Saint-Martin itself. All of them were electrically powered and needed an attendant to operate them.

Monsieur Pamplemousse's knowledge of the inland waterways of France was fairly hazy, but as far as he knew none of the locks were manned during the hours of darkness. He looked at his watch, then fumbled for his shoes. There was only one way to find out for certain. Go there and look for himself.

The main gates to the Marina were still open and as Monsieur Pamplemousse made his way down the cobbled slip road leading to the water his heart sank. There were boats as far as the eye could see. At a rough guess, there must be well over two hundred of all shapes and sizes tied up on either side of the basin.

A line of yellow lamps along the deserted *quai* was still switched on, contrasting with the brighter lights from the streets high up on either side. A few of the boats were showing lights, and from one or two he could hear the sound of a party in full swing, but the majority were in darkness.

A restaurant at the top of a flight of steps to his left was just closing for the night. During the winter months most of its trade probably came from the few resident boat-owners who were tired of cooking in cramped galleys, and they probably ate early. In the summer things would be different. Then it would attract the tourist trade as well.

To his right lay the entrance to the long tunnel which ran

beneath the Place de la Bastille and then followed the line of the Boulevard Richard-Lenoir before finally emerging some two kilometres away near the Place de la République. From there it continued via a series of old-fashioned locks and swing bridges until it reached the basin at La Villette. It was Simenon country, an area of artisans, and popular with film-makers who went there in search of 'atmosphere'.

A red traffic light to the left of the tunnel entrance forbade entry.

The area in front of him was laid out as formal gardens with rose-covered archways, paths and symmetrical rows of low-cut hedges. He could see the mast of a giant model schooner rising up out of what must be a children's play area.

On the cobbled quayside, a sign pointed the way to the Harbour Master's office at the far end, near the entrance to the Seine. The building was in darkness. He would get no help there.

Beyond it, a Métro train rattled across a bridge, its wheels shrieking in protest at the sharp curve which took it into the Quai de la Rapée station.

As he reached the water's edge Monsieur Pamplemousse stood for a moment or two considering what he was looking for. By process of elimination, it was unlikely to be one of the sailing boats moored on his side. Most of them were so large they had been tied up lengthways on to avoid causing an obstruction. They would have far too big a draught for a journey across France by canal. Most likely they had been brought up river from Le Havre to spend the winter inland.

The bulk of the smaller boats were moored on the far side of the Marina. He ran his eye along them. Given the time of the year, it was unlikely that Dubois would be in an open boat, and in view of the weather and some of the currents he must have encountered between canals *en route*, he would have needed something with a fairly powerful motor. A me-dium-size cabin cruiser perhaps, one with an inboard engine. Even so, that still left a wide choice. In their various ways, practically ninety per cent of the craft came into that category. Each had its own mooring position with a selection of utility services it could plug in to.

Suddenly, he felt rather than saw a movement at his side, and his spirits rose. It was Pommes Frites; large as life and in the circumstances, twice as beautiful. If Pommes Frites didn't actually say 'Sssh', he made his meaning very clear as he stretched out on the ground beside his master. Only the faintest movement of his tail betrayed his pleasure.

Monsieur Pamplemousse bent down and gave his friend a pat. Pommes Frites' neck felt cold and damp and he was trembling all over, but whether it was a simple case of cause and effect or sheer excitement it was hard to tell. From the alert expression on his face and from the way he was lying, ears pricked up, nose twitching, legs ready to spring into action at a moment's notice, Monsieur Pamplemousse strongly suspected the latter. He turned to look back at the Marina.

Pommes Frites' gaze was firmly fastened on a boat moored, stern on, almost opposite them on the far side of the basin. It was a motor cruiser some ten metres in length, with a closed-in wheelhouse aft of the forward cabin. Even to Monsieur Pamplemousse's inexpert eyes it looked solid and workman-like compared with those tied up on either side of it. The decks were of varnished teak and there was a businesslike array of radio aerials attached to a stubby mast. From where he was standing it was impossible to see the stern.

Straining his eyes, Monsieur Pamplemousse thought he detected a momentary glimmer of light from inside the wheelhouse, but a second later it disappeared.

He looked to his right and then to his left, trying to decide the best way of getting across to the far side. It was a case of swings and roundabouts. The boat was moored rather nearer the Place de la Bastille than the Seine, but there was another Métro station between the *Place* and the Marina and if they went that way it would mean losing sight of it for a while, then taking a chance that the entrance near the tunnel on the far side was open.

If they went to the left and crossed over via the lock they would be able to keep the boat in view the whole time, but against that they would have to travel much further and then run the risk of being seen as they made their way along the opposite *quai* which looked totally empty and bereft of any kind of shelter.

He tossed a mental coin and chose the first way.

The pavement area above the tunnel was packed with parked cars and they had to squeeze a tortuous path in and out of them. It took rather longer than Monsieur Pamplemousse had bargained for. Worse still, when they finally reached the other side, although the gate at the top of the steps was open, a second one half-way down was securely padlocked. He glanced through the bars at the Marina.

'*Merde!*' Slowly, almost imperceptibly, the boat was edging away from the *quai*. Already there was a good metre between the prow and the mooring post.

Somehow or other they must have been spotted. He could see someone lying prone on the foredeck, inching the boat along by pushing against the one in the next berth. Even from a distance he was clearly recognisable as the man in the photograph.

Signalling Pommes Frites to follow on behind, Monsieur Pamplemousse slowly backed up the steps, keeping as close to the shadow of the wall as possible.

Having reached the top, he set off across the Place de la Bastille as fast as he could go. Although he was acting out of pure instinct, Monsieur Pamplemousse was also aware that Dubois had very little choice in the matter. He was hardly likely to make for the Seine. His exit would be blocked by the lock. If he went through the tunnel he could either hide in there until morning – in which case there would be ample time to bring in reinforcements – or tie up just beyond the far exit near the Place de la République, some two kilometres away.

Given the fact that Dubois would most likely want to put as much distance as he could between himself and his pursuer, the latter course seemed the more likely of the two. If the worse came to the worst, once Dubois reached the far end he could always abandon Madame Grante and make good his escape. The prime object uppermost in Monsieur Pample-mousse's mind as he tried to ignore the agony in his calves was to get there ahead of him.

In the beginning luck was with him. He'd picked a moment when the main stream of traffic was flowing off to his left towards the river and he reached the island in the centre of the *Place* in double quick time. But as he set out to cross to the far side, he encountered a mass of cars and buses sweeping round from the new Opera House. Dodging in and out of it, he left in his wake a cacophony of screaming tyres, horns, shouts, and an ominous dull crunch of metal hitting metal. The insurance companies would be busy in the morning.

As he reached the safety of the wide central reservation which divided the Boulevard Richard Lenoir in two, Mon-sieur Pamplemousse's pace began to slow. It dawned on him that in no way was he going to make the other end of the tunnel before the boat, if indeed he got there at all.

Already his feet felt as though they were made of lead. His heart was pounding, and his temples were beginning to throb.

Pommes Frites had no such worries. He was just getting into his stride. Galloping on ahead, he looked good for another thirty kilometres at least. Clearly, as he stood waiting for his master to catch up, he was anticipating further instruc-tions. Equally clearly, he was going to have to wait awhile.

Monsieur Pamplemousse bent down in a vain effort to touch his toes. Almost immediately he felt a sharp pain in his side. It was nature's warning; the beginnings of a stitch.

He looked around for a taxi, but as always at such mo-ments, there wasn't one in sight, and he certainly didn't intend braving the wrath of those in the *Place* by going back in search of a rank.

After a moment or two, having got his second wind, Mon-sieur Pamplemousse moved off at a slower pace, trying to keep up a steady, if less ambitious jog trot. At least he had a head start, although it was a moot point as to how long that would last once Dubois started the engine and got up speed.

Once upon a time, the central reservation had been open to the sky, the canal itself separating the fourth from the eleventh *arrondissements*. As he skirted round some railings he was reminded of a boat trip he had once taken on the canal with Doucette.

Dotted along the length of the tunnel there were a number of round openings, each about two metres across. Basically intended to provide ventilation, during the daytime they also gave those below the benefit of a series of strange, almost translucent shafts of light. It stuck in his mind because at the time he had tried to capture the effect on film and had wildly misjudged the exposure.

The top of each opening was protected by a domed steel frame covered in thick wire mesh, and these were further screened off from the public by railed-off areas planted with shrubs and roses. During the summer months the holes themselves were scarcely visible.

Monsieur Pamplemousse vaulted over the first set of railings. Ignoring the thorns tearing at his trouser legs, he reached down and tugged at one of the covers. It remained firmly in place. He tried a second one. That showed no sign of movement either. Feeling along the inside of the rim he came across some stout metal cleats let into the concrete.

He ran on to the next enclosure, but once again luck was against him.

The fifth cover shifted slightly when he pulled at it, but it was beyond his strength to lift the frame clear of the stonework. In desperation he looked around for something he could use as a lever, but there was nothing.

Lying prone on the ground, Monsieur Pamplemousse put an ear to the opening and heard the faint chug-chug of an approaching engine. Pommes Frites heard it too and began pawing the ground impatiently.

About half-way along the first leg of the Boulevard, just before the Richard-Lenoir Métro station, Monsieur Pamplemousse found what he was looking for. As he pulled at one of the frames it gave slightly and he heard a splash of falling masonry in the water below.

Gathering all his strength, he made another attempt to shift it and this time managed to lift the metalwork clear of its concrete surround. Bracing himself, he pushed upwards and outwards on the frame as hard as he could and as it rolled over he flung it clear into the nearby shrubs.

Bending down, Monsieur Pamplemousse peered into the darkness below, but it was impossible to make out anything. He took hold of a loose piece of masonry and dropped it through the opening. From the time it took to hit the water he judged the distance to be about five metres at the most. Given the height of the boat, that would make the deck a little over three metres away – always assuming Dubois was steering a course down the middle of the canal, which would be the natural thing to do.

Above the sound of traffic flowing past on either side of the island, he could hear the engine again – much closer this time, and faster.

Monsieur Pamplemousse lowered himself over the edge of the shaft and, as ill luck would have it, caught his jacket on some kind of projection. He felt himself dangling in space, his feet clear of the bottom of the opening. He held his breath as he caught sight of an approaching spotlight. Luckily it was pointing in a downward direction. The water below showed up inky black in its rays. Even if he'd had the strength to lift himself up again, there wasn't time – the boat was almost on him.

In retrospect, although he wouldn't have been prepared to swear on oath that Pommes Frites actually pushed him with intent – giving him the benefit of the doubt, it was probably more a case of the excitement of the chase getting the better of him – the effect was much the same, as some fifty kilograms of bone, muscle and flesh landed on Monsieur Pamplemousse's shoulders.

Even above the roar of the engine echoing around the walls of the cavern-like tunnel, Monsieur Pamplemousse was aware of a rending sound as he parted company with whatever it was that had been holding him back and he felt himself falling.

The next few seconds felt like a clip from some modern 'pop video', the kind where no single image lasted long enough to leave more than a fleeting impression.

As he landed awkwardly on the foredeck he sprawled over on all fours, carried forward by the speed of the boat. He clutched at the mast to stop himself falling over the side, acutely conscious that if his fall had been delayed by even a fraction of a second he might well have been impaled on the end of it.

While he was struggling to regain his balance, he heard a second crash just behind him, followed immediately by the sound of splintering wood.

Once again, viewed in retrospect, it would have been hard to say whether Pommes Frites was in total control of the situation. Inasmuch as he landed fairly and squarely on the middle of the wheelhouse, which was considerably higher than the foredeck, he was luckier than his master, for he had less far to travel. On the other hand, honours were rendered more or less equal when he went straight through the roof.

As his rear end disappeared from view the boat rocked violently and went out of control, heading at speed towards the starboard side of the canal. There was a brief exchange of growls and oaths, followed by a cry of pain, then two splashes in quick succession.

As Monsieur Pamplemousse crawled across the roof of the wheelhouse and lowered himself down through the hole he caught a brief glimpse of two dark shapes in the water. It looked as though the second was gaining rapidly on the first.

There was a crash and the boat rocked even more violently as they struck the granite edge of the towpath a glancing blow. Monsieur Pamplemousse made a grab for the wheel. He had no idea how deep the canal was at that point, and there were better ways of finding out than by sinking.

With his other hand he reached for the throttle control and slowly eased it back, but not before they hit the towpath on the opposite side.

From somewhere astern of the boat he heard a cry of pain. Pommes Frites must have caught up with his quarry. One thing was certain. If he had got his teeth into Dubois there would be no letting go. He would hang on until the bitter end.

Monsieur Pamplemousse eased the throttle lever back still further until they were barely moving, then he tried the door leading to the forward cabin. It was locked. He called out but there was no reply.

For the second time in as many moments the sound of splintering wood echoed round the walls of the chamber.

Monsieur Pamplemousse felt round the edge of the door frame until he found a switch. He clicked it on.

Bathed in the light from a single overhead bulb he saw a figure stretched out on a bunk at the far end. From the way it was lying it was patently obvious why there had been no reply.

10

The Final Print-out

Monsieur Pamplemousse studied a long, hand-written list of 'things to do' as he paused for a moment outside the Director's office, mentally ticking off the items as he went.

JoJo was in his rightful place in Madame Grante's apartment; the stand-by *oiseau* from the pet shop was back with the Director. That in itself hadn't been as easy as it sounded. The first mistake – and one he wouldn't make again in a hurry – had been to let both birds out for their morning fly at the same time. Catching one had been bad enough; catching two was more than one too many. With the early-morning traffic building up behind him in the Rue des Renaudes, the taxi driver had not been pleased at being kept waiting.

On the way back to Madame Grante's apartment he had visited her in hospital. Outwardly at least, she was very little the worse for her experience and, subject to a favourable report from the doctor, she would be going home later that same day.

Before leaving the Rue des Renaudes for good, he had been through the apartment with a fine-tooth comb. Sheets and pillow cases had been taken to the launderette and were freshly ironed, and every last trace of Pommes Frites' hairs had been removed from the carpet and rugs with a vacuum cleaner. JoJo's supplies had been 'doctored' to make it look as though they had never been replenished. Monsieur Pamplemousse was particularly pleased with the last touch. It was what separated the professional from the amateur. He'd very nearly slipped up and filled both water and seed bowl to the brim. The sand on the floor of the cage looked as though it hadn't been touched for days. With luck Madame Grante would have so many other things on her mind she would never know he had been there. Any missing items of food she would put down to her erstwhile lover.

He'd ordered some flowers and a large box of chocolates for the girls in Communications. They should arrive at any moment.

A message of thanks had gone out to Jacques asking when and where he would like to be taken out to dinner. The fact that in the end he'd been able to do without his help was beside the point, there were still things to be done.

Only one vital piece of the jigsaw was missing – the fate of the missing *disques*, and that he could do nothing about.

Suddenly conscious from the odd glances Pommes Frites kept giving him, that he wasn't exactly looking his best, Monsieur Pamplemousse made a half-hearted attempt at straightening his tie, before knocking on the door.

'Aristide!' The Director jumped to his feet and came bounding round his desk as they entered. 'Congratulations!'

Monsieur Pamplemousse gave a shrug. 'It is not quite as satisfactory as I would have wished, *Monsieur*.' Personally he would have awarded himself eight out of ten at the most. Without the vital *disques*, publication of *Le Guide* would have to be delayed indefinitely.

'At least we can sleep safely in our beds from now on. What do you think will happen to him?'

Monsieur Pamplemousse gave another shrug, even more non-committal than the first. How long was a piece of string? It was out of his hands now.

'Time alone will tell, *Monsieur*.'

Like a visiting dignitary inspecting his guard of honour, the Director stood back in order to get a better view of his guests.

'I trust Pommes Frites' head will soon be better.'

'The *vétérinaire* has said the bandages can be removed in a few days.'

'Good. Good. As soon as they are we must make sure he is suitably rewarded.' The Director fastened his gaze on Monsieur Pamplemousse.

'I must say you have surpassed yourself this time, Aristide. Before we go any further I must let you divest yourself of your disguise, although if I may venture one criticism, I doubt if even the most hard done-by of the working classes – an artisan who has seen his livelihood submerged beneath a tidal wave of cheap imported Japanese goods, or someone practising what has become a dying trade, a wheelwright, perhaps, or soothsayer – would hardly venture forth knowing there was a large tear in his trouser leg. As for the jacket lapels hanging by a thread, do you not think that is a trifle over the top?'

'I am afraid, *Monsieur*, I had a little accident. I was climbing through a ventilation shaft and it got caught in a projection of some kind. As for the trousers, I had an encounter with some rose bushes. I will ask Madame Pamplemousse to see what she can do before I return them.'

The Director stared at him, glassy-eyed. 'You mean that is my suit you are wearing?'

'*Oui, Monsieur*, it is the one you were kind enough to lend me.'

'But that was one of my best suits, Pamplemousse. It came with a ten-year guarantee!'

'In that case, *Monsieur*, there is no problem. You have good cause to complain.'

'They are not designed for use below ground, Pamplemousse,' said the Director severely, 'least of all in *les égouts*!'

Monsieur Pamplemousse took a deep breath. He could see he was in for a difficult time. 'It was not in the sewers, *Monsieur*,' he began. 'It was in the Canal Saint-Martin . . . '

'Canals, sewers, they are all one and the same, Pamplemousse.' The Director sounded less than mollified.

'Perhaps, *Monsieur*, you could catch Madame Grante while she is in a good mood. In the circumstances she can hardly turn down a claim for expenses.'

'Hmmph. You don't know how much it cost. She will need to be in a very good mood indeed. I suggest you choose something a little less costly for the time being – you will find a sports jacket somewhere in the wardrobe.'

'You are very kind, *Monsieur*.' Before the Director had time to comment further, Monsieur Pamplemousse disappeared into the other room. Ever sensitive to the atmosphere, Pommes Frites followed on behind.

When they returned, the Director was busying himself in front of his drinks cupboard, opening some wine. He looked in a better mood. Monsieur Pamplemousse caught a glimpse of the label on the bottle. It was a Bâtard-Montrachet from Remoissenet, an '83. It must have been left over from the launch party. Perks were not confined to the office staff making free telephone calls.

'I have put another bottle on one side for you, Aristide. I think you deserve it.' The Director must have read his thoughts.

Monsieur Pamplemousse murmured his appreciation as he took a large Burgundy glass and held it to his nose. So much had happened it hardly seemed possible that only a few days had passed since he had last tasted it. 'Twice in one week is a very great privilege, *Monsieur*. It is not often I am able to afford such nectar.'

The Director brushed aside the compliment. 'Good wine is never expensive, Aristide. Only bad wine is expensive.' He crossed the room and opened one of the french windows leading to his balcony.

'I do believe we are in for a change in the weather. Look, the sun is shining.' He stepped outside and took in a deep draught of fresh air. 'A perfect spring day at last!'

Monsieur Pamplemousse joined his chief on the balcony. All around there was the hum of traffic. The Boules players were still at it.

'I am dying to hear everything. Tell me about Madame Grante, how is she? What did she have to say when you found her?'

Monsieur Pamplemousse hesitated. The truth was that in the event it had all been strangely formal. When he removed her gag she had said 'Monsieur Pamplemousse' and he had said 'Madame Grante'. They might have just bumped into each other in the street. Afterwards, on the way to the hospital, he had held her hand and she had said his name again.

'She is little the worse for her adventure, *Monsieur*. It is largely a matter of getting her circulation back. When I went to see her she was already asking about the P39s, wondering if they were beginning to pile up. I did my best to reassure her.'

'Ah, with some people, Pamplemousse, recovery is a mixed blessing. Tell me, was she . . . was she complete? Did she have her full complement of digits? There was nothing missing, I trust?'

'As far as I could tell, *Monsieur*, Madame Grante was complete in every detail. Those that were visible. I cannot, of course, vouch for what lay or did not lie beneath the sheets.'

The Director had the grace to blush. 'You know what the mail is like these days, Aristide. There might have been something still in the post. I wouldn't have forgiven myself if anything had happened.

'Has she . . . has she recovered in other ways?'

'It is hard to say, *Monsieur*. Time alone will tell.'

'I wonder what made her do it?'

'Love clouds judgement, *Monsieur*.'

'Do you think there was any love on his part, or was it totally a matter of expediency?'

'Perhaps a little of each.' Secretly, Monsieur Pamplemousse found himself hoping there was a lot of the first. It would be unbearably sad if there wasn't.

'It is certainly hard to picture.'

'*La nuit, toutes les chattes sont grises, Monsieur*. They say that all cats are grey in the dark.'

'Do you really believe that, Pamplemousse?'

'*Non, Monsieur*.' Monsieur Pamplemousse shook his head. 'No, I have never believed that.'

'I am pleased to hear it. Were that true there would be little hope for mankind.'

Monsieur Pamplemousse couldn't help thinking it would also mean an end to romance. He took in the scene before them. The Eiffel Tower to their left, in front of them the Seine, and beyond that the Grand Palais and the Tuileries. On the horizon there was the Sacré-Coeur to remind him that he would soon be home again. The whole added up to a feeling of permanence.

The Director read his thoughts.

'France may be a country divided into fifty-five million inhabitants, Aristide, but with all our faults, God loves the French best. We don't have a future, we have a destiny, a destiny rich in memories of the past. We are indeed a favoured nation. That is my belief.'

Monsieur Pamplemousse resisted the temptation to remark that the poet Péguy had thought of it first. The Director was definitely feeling better. He was about to enter one of his Napoleonic moods. It was one of the great disadvantages of being situated within sight of the Emperor's tomb. He chose the line of least resistance.

'It is a very reassuring view, *Monsieur*. It makes it even harder to believe that such a small mistake made by one person so many years ago could have caused so much disruption.'

'No, Aristide, there I beg to differ. It was not a small mistake, it was a blatant and unforgivable act of deception, one which brought dishonour not only to his calling, but to his father's memory as well. It had to be stamped on.

'Curnonsky, the Prince of gastronomes, once said: "Never eat the left leg of a partridge, for that is the leg it sits on." A counsel of perfection perhaps, but one must have standards. Gastronomy is not just a matter of pots and pans, it is also a mental attitude.

'We must maintain our standards. I have read that there are more nutrients in a cornflake packet than there are in the actual cornflakes themselves. There are undoubtedly people out there who are only too willing to take advantage of that fact. We must guard against the erosion of our taste-buds in the name of convenience. The world is full of people who care so little about standards they would be only too willing to meet the demands of those who eat to live rather than live to eat in order to make a profit.

'Do you wish to eat neurotic tasteless birds, brought up on antibiotics, killed before they have acquired any taste, frozen

solid until they are like rocks before being dumped into a
freezer cabinet, with nothing left to thaw out except water?
Or do you want to eat birds which have been brought up on a
proper diet of maize and dairy products; chicken which taste
as though they have led a happy life?

'It may sound a small matter, Pamplemousse, but it is the
tip of the iceberg. In the end it is a matter of how you want
things to be. What kind of world you wish to inhabit. That
was the question uppermost in my mind that evening many
years ago, and once I had posed the question, I had no doubt
in my mind as to the answer.'

The Director was right, of course. Monsieur Pamplemousse would have done exactly the same thing in his place,
otherwise what was he doing in his present job?

'And now, Aristide, for my little morsel of news.' The
Director turned and led the way back into his room. 'I think I
may say with all due modesty that I have achieved something
of a breakthrough myself. When I woke this morning and
found you had returned the *oiseau* to my office, I must say I
felt somewhat piqued, but at long last patience has reaped its
due reward. Somewhat late in the day the *oiseau* and I have
established a rapport. Conversation is limited at present to a
few basic pleasantries, and the language is, I fear, not all that
one might expect from a creature who has spent most of its
life either in the nest or in the company of a maiden lady, but
who knows where it may lead, perhaps even to the recovery
of the missing *disques*?'

Crossing to where the bird cage was standing, the Director
removed the cloth with a flourish.

'*Comment ça va*, JoJo?'

The effect, as far as at least one member of his audience of
two was concerned, was no less magical than it would have
been had they been watching the great Robert-Houdin per-
forming at the peak of his career.

'*Comment ça va*, JoJo?' The Director's words were echoed
by a smaller, though in its way, and size for size, hardly less
powerful voice. There then followed a stream of expletives
which would not have disgraced a stevedore who had suffered

the misfortune of having a bulk container break loose from a dockside crane and land on his foot.

'*Merde!*' Monsieur Pamplemousse involuntarily added his quota to JoJo's list of adjectives as the truth of the matter sank in. Somehow or other he must have got the two birds mixed up. His heart sank as he looked at his watch. In all probability Madame Grante would be getting ready to go home by now – if she wasn't already on her way. There wasn't a moment to be lost.

'I am sorry, *Monsieur*. I shouldn't have inflicted JoJo on you. I will remove the cage at once. In any case I must return him to Madame Grante.'

'I shall miss it, Aristide.' The Director looked genuinely sorry. 'Birds are strange creatures. They are like women. Who knows what goes on in their minds?'

Monsieur Pamplemousse decided to strike while the iron was hot.

'*Monsieur*, I know someone whose *oiseau* has recently received a great shock. In all probability it has temporarily lost the power of speech. Given your success with JoJo . . .'

'You're a good fellow, Aristide. I don't know what I would have done without you these last few days.' The Director crossed to his drinks cupboard. 'You must have two bottles of wine. I insist.'

If Monsieur Pamplemousse had a twinge of conscience, it was only momentary. After all he had been through, he felt as though a whole vintage would not have come amiss. He paused at the door.

'I shall be back very soon, *Monsieur*.'

It was with a feeling of *déjà vu* that Monsieur Pamplemousse climbed out of a taxi in the Rue des Renaudes for what he fervently hoped was the very last time plus one. He was beginning to get the feeling that he was somehow caught up in an avant-garde play, doomed to trudge the streets of Paris for ever carrying a bird cage as a penance for past misdemeanours. His mood transmitted itself to his companions. Pommes Frites clearly felt much the same way about things as he gazed gloomily up and down the street, and the object of the exercise, JoJo himself, had remained mute for the whole of the journey.

As they paused outside the entrance to Madame Grante's apartment, Monsieur Pamplemousse felt in his pocket for the keys, then stifled an oath. In his anxiety to restore the status quo and return things to normal he'd put them back in Madame Grante's drawer at the office. He turned and waved, but the taxi had already disappeared round the nearest corner.

It was then that he made his second mistake. Truly, misfortunes never came singly. Glancing towards the upper floors of the block he caught sight of Madame Grante looking out of her window. She must have beaten him to it. It was also abundantly clear from the look on her face that she had seen everything, including the cage.

He made his way into the entrance hall and pressed the button for her apartment. He would have to put a brave face on things. In response to a buzz, he pushed open the inner door, signalling at the same time for Pommes Frites to remain where he was. Pommes Frites was only too pleased to obey.

The lift was waiting. On the way up it struck Monsieur Pamplemousse that it seemed to be going faster than usual. The door to the apartment opened before he had a chance to touch the bell-push.

'Madame Grante . . . I know you are not going to believe this . . .'

'In that case, Monsieur Pamplemousse, why bother to tell me.' It was a statement rather than a question.

'As you may have gathered, when we became alarmed for your safety I visited your apartment.'

'I trust Pommes Frites did not come too. JoJo is terrified of dogs. He either goes berserk or else he goes into hiding. Once, when I had a friend for *déjeuner*, he hid in a fold of the curtains. It took me until the evening to find him.'

Monsieur Pamplemousse held up the cage. 'I realised that, Madame Grante. Which is why I thought it best to remove him to a place of safety. JoJo has been in good hands. He has been staying with the Director. The one in your cage is merely a stand-in.'

As JoJo jumped from his perch and clung to the bars of the cage nearest Madame Grante, Monsieur Pamplemousse had a sudden thought. 'I believe *Monsieur le Directeur* has been trying to teach him a few new words. He seemed very pleased with the result.'

It was an insurance policy. There was no knowing what the real JoJo might say once he found himself back in familiar surroundings.

'Perhaps you would like to change the *oiseaux* over. I'm sure you are much better at it than I am.'

He wondered if Madame Grante would invite him in, but she made no attempt. Instead, she disappeared for a moment or two before returning with the cage containing its rightful occupant. In her other hand she held a large manila envelope.

'This is for you. I suggest you open it when you get back to the office.'

Monsieur Pamplemousse obediently relieved her of both. He held his breath. Already he could hear JoJo holding forth.

'I believe you have something of mine?' said Madame Grante.

'I do?'

'I left it under my pillow.'

It definitely wasn't his day. Putting the cage down for a moment, he felt for his wallet, then handed Madame Grante the photograph. She took it without a word.

'I am very sorry.' Monsieur Pamplemousse found himself at a loss for words. 'It must have been a very distressing experience for you. Did you and he . . . ?' The words slipped out before he could stop them.

'Did we what, Monsieur Pamplemousse?'

'*Pardon, Madame.*' It was unforgivable. Not at all what he had meant to say.

'We had a wonderful time together, while it lasted.'

As she closed the door he saw there were tears in her eyes.

On the way down the lift seemed to have reverted to its normal slow pace again. What was it Proust had said? The true paradises are paradises we have lost.

✻   ✻   ✻

The Director removed two film-wrapped *disques* from the envelope and gazed at them. 'Do you mean to say, Pample-mousse, these were hidden in the *oiseau*'s cage all the time? I can hardly believe it.'

'I could hardly believe it myself, *Monsieur*. It is the old story of the man on the building site who every day was seen removing a brick in a wheelbarrow. No one bothered to challenge him for taking just one brick. It wasn't until it was too late that they discovered he was really stealing wheelbar-rows.'

The Director frowned. 'I'm not sure that I follow you.'

'We thought our man was after the bird, whereas in fact what he wanted to get hold of was the right cage.'

'The *right* cage, Pamplemousse? I still don't understand what you are getting at.'

Realising that he was about to get himself into deep water, Monsieur Pamplemousse hastily changed tack. 'What I am saying, *Monsieur*, is that he must have hidden the *disques* in JoJo's cage at some point. According to her note, it wasn't until Madame Grante returned home and removed the sheet of sanded paper in order to clean it out properly that she discovered them. They fitted almost exactly into the bottom of the tray.'

Fortunately the Director had other things to think about. 'It is a great weight off my mind, Aristide.' He picked up the telephone. 'I must warn the printers to stand by. With luck, the first copies of *Le Guide* should start rolling off the presses tonight. Review copies will be despatched immediately they become available.'

It seemed a good moment to leave, but as Monsieur Pamplemousse turned to go the Director waved him to re-main.

'I have something addressed to you, Aristide. It came through on the computer just before you arrived back. It appears to be in some kind of code.'

Monsieur Pamplemousse reached across and took a sheet of computer print-out from the Director. As always, the length of the message bore no relation to the amount of paper. It was short and to the point: MORE RAIN IS FORECAST. AMPLE FUNDS ARE AVAILABLE IF YOU WISH TO CASH YOUR CHEQUE. BANK OF PASSY. Ten out of ten to Martine for persistence.

The Director put a hand over the mouthpiece of the receiver. 'What do you think it means, Aristide? Can it be that someone else has already entered the system?'

'Perhaps the engineers are conducting some kind of tests, *Monsieur*. I will investigate the matter straight away.'

'Please do, Aristide, there's a good fellow. And don't forget your bottles of wine. They are with Véronique.'

Monsieur Pamplemousse hesitated at the door. 'I have a little something for you, *Monsieur*. It is also with Véronique.'

It wasn't a bad swop – two bottles of Bâtard-Montrachet for one *perruche*. At least it solved the problem of what to do with JoJo's stand-in.

Back at his desk, Monsieur Pamplemousse found another note awaiting him. This time it was from Jacques. He ran his eyes down it.

' . . . A few years later he tried again with a restaurant boat on the river but someone shopped him. After that he drifted for a while, worked as a radio operator on board ship; he even tried his luck working the canals in the Paris area, but eventually he gave that up and returned to Belfort. Computers were coming into their own, and because of his experience as a radio operator, he landed a job with Poulanc . . . ' Congratulations followed, then: 'Next time, be a good fellow and bring us in earlier. It'll save an awful lot of tedious explanations.'

Next time! Monsieur Pamplemousse gazed out of the window for a moment or two. He hoped there would never be a 'next time'. With luck, Dubois should be out of the way for some while to come and would have learned his lesson. He wondered if, during his time in Paris, he had ever come near *Le Guide*'s offices. If he'd seen the Director driving out through the gates in his usual splendour, the grievance he had been nursing over the years would have come flooding back, enlarged out of all proportion. Probably when his journeyings on the Seine took him past the Esplanade des Invalides he'd taken to thinking out ways of getting his revenge. It was hard to imagine the surprise he must have felt when suddenly, years later, the Director turned up out of the blue at the Poulanc factory.

Monsieur Pamplemousse gave a sigh. It all seemed academic now. Around him the rest of the staff were rushing about their work as news filtered through that all was well again.

Monsieur Pamplemousse picked up the telephone. He suddenly felt very flat.

Pile ou face? Heads or tails?

He took out a coin and tossed it. Tails. He dialled a number.

'Couscous. I have finished what I was doing. I shall be home this evening.'

'*Oh, là! là!*' Doucette sounded flustered. If only he had phoned earlier. Her sister was already hard at work preparing the evening meal. *Tripe à la mode de Caen*. They were having it for the simple reason that Agathe knew he didn't like it.

Monsieur Pamplemousse felt tempted to say that an even simpler reason why he didn't like the dish was because of the way Agathe made it. Tripe needed to be cooked for a long time, preferably in a casserole which had been hermetically sealed with flour and water paste. If you didn't, it was a sure recipe for indigestion. Agathe couldn't be bothered with such niceties, and he almost always suffered accordingly.

'We have plenty. It can be divided. You will be more than welcome.'

'No, no, Couscous, I shall be all right, really I shall. Tomorrow night we can go out and make up for it.

'You, too, *ma chérie.*'

Clearing the call, he allowed all of two seconds to elapse, then he dialled Martine's number.

'Bank of Passy? I have a cheque I wish to cash. What time do you close?'

'We are open until late this evening.'

'In that case I will be with you as soon as possible.'

'Would you like to know what I have planned?'

MONSIEUR PAMPLEMOUSSE INVESTIGATES

'Tell me.'

'*Moules aux amandes.*'

Mussels with almonds. That was more like it. He felt his mouth watering at the thought. It was a Basque speciality. The last time he'd tasted it had been in a little restaurant in Saint-Jean-de-Luz. It had been helped on its way with a *pousse-rapière* beforehand – Armagnac, sparkling white wine and a slice of orange. The memory lingered.

'And after that?'

'*Poularde en demi-deuil.*'

'Aaaah!' Monsieur Pamplemousse felt his salivary glands begin to work overtime at the mere mention of the name. It was a dish made famous by one of the *Mères Lyonnaises*. Chicken with slices of truffle placed in splits between the skin and the breast. It was an apt name – chicken in partial mourning.

'And the *poularde* is from where?'

'Bresse, of course!'

'Of course! Where else?' In the circumstances it couldn't possibly be otherwise.

The bird would be stuffed with sausage meat mixed with white of egg, cream and breadcrumbs, then it would be poached in a *court-bouillon* containing leeks, carrots, turnips and celery. It was *not* something his mother had ever cooked. Even on fête days, truffles had been way beyond their reach.

'Then some cheese. I have managed to get something special from near home which you may like to try.

'And to finish, there are orange sorbets . . . '

'Served inside the orange with meringue on top?'

She laughed. 'There are other ways?'

'I will see you soon. May I bring the wine? I have something I think you will appreciate.'

Monsieur Pamplemousse suddenly realised how hungry he felt. Even so, he knew someone who must be feeling even hungrier.

'May I also bring Pommes Frites?'

'Of course. I will lay another place.'

Pommes Frites pricked up his ears at the sound of his

174

name. Given the various other evocative words he had overheard during the course of the conversation, words like
poularde and *Bresse*, add to them the look of anticipation on
his master's face – a look he knew only too well – and it all
sounded distinctly promising.

He stood up as his master replaced the receiver. It was time
to reorganise his filing system. Certain smells could now be
relegated to the archives; new ones would soon be taking
their place.

And the very nice thing about that, he decided as he followed Monsieur Pamplemousse down the corridor and into a
room at the far end, was that he would be sharing them with
the person who meant most to him in the world.

Only one thing puzzled Pommes Frites. Why on earth at
such a moment waste valuable time bothering to shave? There
were some things about his master he would never understand.